GIRL WITH A
PEARL EARRING

Tracy Chevalier

Girl With a
Pearl Earring

WheeleR
PUBLISHING, INC.
ROCKLAND, MA
★ AN AMERICAN COMPANY ★

Published in Large Print by arrangement with Dutton, a member of Penguin Putnam Inc. in the United States and Canada.

Wheeler Large Print Book Series.

Set in 16 pt Plantin.

Library of Congress Cataloging-in-Publication Data

Chevalier, Tracy.
 Girl with a pearl earring / Tracy Chevalier.
  p. (large print) cm.(Wheeler large print book series)
 ISBN 1-56895-850-1 (hardcover)
 1. Vermeer, Johannes, 1632-1675—Fiction. 2. Artist's models—Netherlands—Delft—Fiction. 3. Women domestics—Netherlands—Delft—Fiction. 4. Delft (Netherlands)—Fiction. 5. Large type books. I. Title. II. Series

[PS3553.H4367G57   2000b]
813'.54—dc21
                                                                    99-086686
                                                                         CIP

For my father

1664

My mother did not tell me they were coming. Afterwards she said she did not want me to appear nervous. I was surprised, for I thought she knew me well. Strangers would think I was calm. I did not cry as a baby. Only my mother would note the tightness along my jaw, the widening of my already wide eyes.

I was chopping vegetables in the kitchen when I heard voices outside our front door—a woman's, bright as polished brass, and a man's, low and dark like the wood of the table I was working on. They were the kind of voices we heard rarely in our house. I could hear rich carpets in their voices, books and pearls and fur.

I was glad that earlier I had scrubbed the front steps so hard.

My mother's voice—a cooking pot, a flagon—approached from the front room. They were coming to the kitchen. I pushed the leeks I had been chopping into place, then set the knife on the table, wiped my hands on my apron and pressed my lips together to smooth them.

My mother appeared in the doorway, her eyes two warnings. Behind her the woman had to duck her head because she was so tall, taller than the man following her.

All of our family, even my father and brother, were small.

The woman looked as if she had been blown about by the wind, although it was a calm day. Her cap was askew so that tiny blond curls escaped and hung about her forehead like bees which she swatted at impatiently several times. Her collar needed straightening and was not as crisp as it could be. She pushed her gray mantle back from her shoulders, and I saw then that under her dark blue dress a baby was growing. It would arrive by the year's end, or before.

The woman's face was like an oval serving plate, flashing at times, dull at others. Her eyes were two light brown buttons, a color I had rarely seen coupled with blond hair. She made a show of watching me hard, but could not fix her attention on me, her eyes darting about the room.

"This is the girl, then," she said abruptly.

"This is my daughter, Griet," my mother replied. I nodded respectfully to the man and woman.

"Well. She's not very big. Is she strong enough?" As the woman turned to look at the man, a fold of her mantle caught the handle of the knife I had been using, knocking it off the table so that it spun across the floor.

The woman cried out.

4

"Catharina," the man said calmly. He spoke her name as if he held cinnamon in his mouth. The woman stopped, making an effort to quiet herself.

I stepped over and picked up the knife, polishing the blade on my apron before placing it back on the table. The knife had brushed against the vegetables. I set a piece of carrot back in its place.

The man was watching me, his eyes grey like the sea. He had a long, angular face, and his expression was steady, in contrast to his wife's, which flickered like a candle. He had no beard or moustache, and I was glad, for it gave him a clean appearance. He wore a black cloak over his shoulders, a white shirt, and a fine lace collar. His hat pressed into hair the red of brick washed by rain.

"What have you been doing here, Griet?" he asked.

I was surprised by the question but knew enough to hide it. "Chopping vegetables, sir. For the soup."

I always laid vegetables out in a circle, each with its own section like a slice of pie. There were five slices: red cabbage, onions, leeks, carrots, and turnips. I had used a knife edge to shape each slice, and placed a carrot disc in the center.

The man tapped his finger on the table. "Are they laid out in the order in which they will go into the soup?" he suggested, studying the circle.

"No, sir." I hesitated. I could not say why

I had laid out the vegetables as I did. I simply set them as I felt they should be, but I was too frightened to say so to a gentleman.

"I see you have separated the whites," he said, indicating the turnips and onions. "And then the orange and the purple, they do not sit together. Why is that?" He picked up a shred of cabbage and a piece of carrot and shook them like dice in his hand.

I looked at my mother, who nodded slightly.

"The colors fight when they are side by side, sir."

He arched his eyebrows, as if he had not expected such a response. "And do you spend much time setting out the vegetables before you make the soup?"

"Oh no, sir," I replied, confused. I did not want him to think I was idle.

From the corner of my eye I saw a movement. My sister, Agnes, was peering round the doorpost and had shaken her head at my response. I did not often lie. I looked down.

The man turned his head slightly and Agnes disappeared. He dropped the pieces of carrot and cabbage into their slices. The cabbage shred fell partly into the onions. I wanted to reach over and tease it into place. I did not, but he knew that I wanted to. He was testing me.

"That's enough prattle," the woman declared. Though she was annoyed with his attention to me, it was me she frowned at. "Tomorrow, then?" She looked at the man before sweeping out of the room, my mother behind her. The man glanced once more at what was to be the soup, then nodded at me and followed the women.

When my mother returned I was sitting by the vegetable wheel. I waited for her to speak. She was hunching her shoulders as if against a winter chill, though it was summer and the kitchen was hot.

"You are to start tomorrow as their maid. If you do well, you will be paid eight stuivers a day. You will live with them."

I pressed my lips together.

"Don't look at me like that, Griet," my mother said. "We have to, now your father has lost his trade."

"Where do they live?"

"On the Oude Langendijck, where it inter-sects with the Molenpoort."

"Papists' corner? They're Catholic?"

"You can come home Sundays. They have agreed to that." My mother cupped her hands around the turnips, scooped them up along with some of the cabbage and onions and dropped them into the pot of water waiting on the fire. The pie slices I had made so carefully were ruined.

I climbed the stairs to see my father. He was sitting at the front of the attic by the window, where the light touched his face. It was the closest he came now to seeing.

Father had been a tile painter, his fingers still stained blue from painting cupids, maids, soldiers, ships, children, fish, flowers, animals onto white tiles, glazing them, firing them, selling them. One day the kiln exploded, taking his eyes and his trade. He was the lucky one—two other men died.

I sat next to him and held his hand.

"I heard," he said before I could speak. "I heard everything." His hearing had taken the strength from his missing eyes.

I could not think of anything to say that would not sound reproachful.

"I'm sorry, Griet. I would like to have done better for you." The place where his eyes had been, where the doctor had sewn shut the skin, looked sorrowful. "But he is a good gentleman, and fair. He will treat you well." He said nothing about the woman.

"How can you be sure of this, Father? Do you know him?"

"Don't you know who he is?"

"No."

"Do you remember the painting we saw in the Town Hall a few years ago, which van Ruijven was displaying after he bought it? It was a view of Delft, from the Rotterdam and Schiedam Gates. With the sky that took up so much of the painting, and the sunlight on some of the buildings."

"And the paint had sand in it to make the brickwork and the roofs look rough," I added. "And there were long shadows in the water, and tiny people on the shore nearest us."

"That's the one." Father's sockets widened

8

as if he still had eyes and was looking at the painting again.

I remembered it well, remembered thinking that I had stood at the very spot many times and never seen Delft the way the painter had.

"That man was van Ruijven?"

"The patron?" Father chuckled. "No, no, child, not him. That was the painter, Vermeer. That was Johannes Vermeer and his wife. You're to clean his studio."

To the few things I was taking with me my mother added another cap, collar and apron so that each day I could wash one and wear the other, and would always look clean. She also gave me an ornamental tortoiseshell comb, shaped like a shell, that had been my grandmother's and was too fine for a maid to wear, and a prayer book I could read when I needed to escape the Catholicism around me.

As we gathered my things she explained why I was to work for the Vermeers. "You know that your new master is headman of the Guild of St. Luke, and was when your father had his accident last year?"

I nodded, still shocked that I was to work for such an artist.

"The Guild looks after its own, as best it can. Remember the box your father gave money to every week for years? That money goes to masters in need, as we are now. But it goes only so far, you see, especially now with Frans in his apprenticeship and no money coming in. We have no choice. We won't take public charity, not if we can manage without. Then your father heard that your new master was looking for a maid who could clean his studio without moving anything, and he put forward your name, thinking that as headman, and knowing our circumstances, Vermeer would be likely to try to help."

I sifted through what she had said. "How do you clean a room without moving anything?"

"Of course you must move things, but you must find a way to put them back exactly so it looks as if nothing has been disturbed. As you do for your father now that he cannot see."

After my father's accident we had learned to place things where he always knew to find them. It was one thing to do this for a blind man, though. Quite another for a man with a painter's eyes.

Agnes said nothing to me after the visit. When I got into bed next to her that night she remained silent, though she did not turn her back to me. She lay gazing at the ceiling. Once I had blown out the candle it was so dark I could see nothing. I turned towards her.

"You know I don't want to leave. I have to."

Silence.

"We need the money. We have nothing now that Father can't work."

"Eight stuivers a day isn't such a lot of money." Agnes had a hoarse voice, as if her throat were covered with cobwebs.

"It will keep the family in bread. And a bit of cheese. That's not so little."

"I'll be all alone. You're leaving me all alone. First Frans, then you."

Of all of us Agnes had been the most upset when Frans left the previous year. He and she had always fought like cats but she sulked for days once he was gone. At ten she was the youngest of us three children, and had never before known a time when Frans and I were not there.

"Mother and Father will still be here. And I'll visit on Sundays. Besides, it was no surprise when Frans went." We had known for years that our brother would start his apprenticeship when he turned thirteen. Our father had saved hard to pay the apprentice fee, and talked endlessly of how Frans would learn another aspect of the trade, then come back and they would set up a tile factory together.

Now our father sat by the window and never spoke of the future.

After the accident Frans had come home for two days. He had not visited since. The last time I saw him I had gone to the factory across town where he was apprenticed. He looked exhausted and had burns up and down his arms from pulling tiles from the kiln. He told me he worked from dawn until so late that at times he was too tired even to eat. "Father never told me it would be this bad," he muttered resentfully. "He always said his apprenticeship was the making of him."

"Perhaps it was," I replied. "It made him what he is now."

When I was ready to leave the next morning my father shuffled out to the front step, feeling his way along the wall. I hugged my mother and Agnes. "Sunday will come in no time," my mother said.

My father handed me something wrapped in a handkerchief. "To remind you of home," he said. "Of us."

It was my favorite tile of his. Most of his tiles we had at home were faulty in some way—chipped or cut crookedly, or the picture was blurred because the kiln had been too hot. This one, though, my father kept specially for us. It was a simple picture of two small figures, a boy and an older girl. They were not playing as children usually did in tiles. They were simply walking along, and were like Frans and me whenever we walked together—clearly our father had thought of us as he painted it. The boy was a little ahead of the girl but had turned back to say something. His face was mischievous, his hair messy. The girl wore her cap as I wore mine, not as most other girls did, with the ends tied under their chins or behind their necks.

12

I favored a white cap that folded in a wide brim around my face, covering my hair completely and hanging down in points on each side of my face so that from the side my expression was hidden. I kept the cap stiff by boiling it with potato peelings.

I walked away from our house, carrying my things tied up in an apron. It was still early—our neighbors were throwing buckets of water onto their steps and the street in front of their houses, and scrubbing them clean. Agnes would do that now, as well as many of my other tasks. She would have less time to play in the street and along the canals. Her life was changing too.

People nodded at me and watched curiously as I passed. No one asked where I was going or called out kind words. They did not need to—they knew what happened to families when a man lost his trade. It would be something to discuss later—young Griet become a maid, her father brought the family low. They would not gloat, however. The same thing could easily happen to them.

I had walked along that street all my life, but had never been so aware that my back was to my home. When I reached the end and turned out of sight of my family, though, it became a little easier to walk steadily and look around me. The morning was still cool, the sky a flat grey-white pulled close over Delft like a sheet, the summer sun not yet high enough to burn it away. The canal I walked along was a mirror of white light tinged with green. As the sun grew brighter the canal would darken to the color of moss.

Frans, Agnes, and I used to sit along that canal and throw things in—pebbles, sticks, once a broken tile—and imagine what they might touch on the bottom—not fish, but creatures from our imagination, with many eyes, scales, hands and fins. Frans thought up the most interesting monsters. Agnes was the most frightened. I always stopped the game, too inclined to see things as they were to be able to think up things that were not.

There were a few boats on the canal, moving towards Market Square. It was not market day, however, when the canal was so full you couldn't see the water. One boat was carrying river fish for the stalls at Jeronymous Bridge. Another sat low on the water, loaded with bricks. The man poling the boat called out a greeting to me. I merely nodded and lowered my head so that the edge of my cap hid my face.

I crossed a bridge over the canal and turned into the open space of Market Square, even then busy with people crisscrossing it on their way to some task—buying meat at the Meat Hall, or bread at the baker's, taking wood to be weighed at the Weigh House. Children ran errands for their parents, apprentices for their masters, maids for their households. Horses and carts clattered across the stones. To my right was the Town Hall, with its gilded front and white marble faces gazing down from the keystones above the windows. To my

14

left was the New Church, where I had been baptized sixteen years before. Its tall, narrow tower made me think of a stone birdcage. Father had taken us up it once. I would never forget the sight of Delft spread below us, each narrow brick house and steep red roof and green waterway and city gate marked forever in my mind, tiny and yet distinct. I asked my father then if every Dutch city looked like that, but he did not know. He had never visited any other city, not even The Hague, two hours away on foot.

I walked to the center of the square. There the stones had been laid to form an eight-pointed star set inside a circle. Each point aimed towards a different part of Delft. I thought of it as the very center of the town, and as the center of my life. Frans and Agnes and I had played in that star since we were old enough to run to the market. In our favorite game, one of us chose a point and one of us named a thing—a stork, a church, a wheelbarrow, a flower—and we ran in that direction looking for that thing. We had explored most of Delft that way.

One point, however, we had never followed. I had never gone to Papists' Corner, where the Catholics lived. The house where I was to work was just ten minutes from home, the time it took a pot of water to boil, but I had never passed by it.

I knew no Catholics. There were not so many in Delft, and none in our street or in the shops we used. It was not that we avoided them, but they kept to themselves. They were tolerated in Delft, but were expected not to parade their faith openly. They held their services privately, in modest places that did not look like churches from the outside.

My father had worked with Catholics and told me they were no different from us. If anything they were less solemn. They liked to eat and drink and sing and game. He said this almost as if he envied them.

I followed that point of the star now, walking across the square more slowly than everyone else, for I was reluctant to leave its familiarity. I crossed the bridge over the canal and turned left up the Oude Langendijck. On my left the canal ran parallel to the street, separating it from Market Square.

At the intersection with the Molenpoort, four girls were sitting on a bench beside an open door of a house. They were arranged in order of size, from the oldest, who looked to be about Agnes' age, to the youngest, who was probably about four. One of the middle girls held a baby in her lap—a large baby, who was probably already crawling and would soon be ready to walk.

Five children, I thought. And another expected.

The oldest was blowing bubbles through a scallop shell fixed to the end of a hollowed stick, very like one my father had made for us. The others were jumping up and popping the bubbles as they appeared. The girl with the baby in her lap could not move much, catching

16

few bubbles although she was seated next to the bubble blower. The youngest at the end was the furthest away and the smallest, and had no chance to reach the bubbles. The second youngest was the quickest, darting after the bubbles and clapping her hands around them. She had the brightest hair of the four, red like the dry brick wall behind her. The youngest and the girl with the baby both had curly blond hair like their mother's, while the eldest's was the same dark red as her father's.

I watched the girl with the bright hair swat at the bubbles, popping them just before they broke on the damp grey and white tiles set diagonally in rows before the house. She will be a handful, I thought. "You'd best pop them before they reach the ground," I said. "Else those tiles will have to be scrubbed again."

The eldest girl lowered the pipe. Four sets of eyes stared at me with the same gaze that left no doubt they were sisters. I could see various features of their parents in them—grey eyes here, light brown eyes there, angular faces, impatient movements.

"Are you the new maid?" the eldest asked.

"We were told to watch out for you," the bright redhead interrupted before I could reply.

"Cornelia, go and get Tanneke," the eldest said to her.

"You go, Aleydis," Cornelia in turn ordered the youngest, who gazed at me with wide grey eyes but did not move.

"*I'll* go." The eldest must have decided my arrival was important after all.

"No, *I'll* go." Cornelia jumped up and ran ahead of her older sister, leaving me alone with the two quieter girls.

I looked at the squirming baby in the girl's lap. "Is that your brother or your sister?"

"Brother," the girl replied in a soft voice like a feather pillow. "His name is Johannes. Never call him Jan." She said the last words as if they were a familiar refrain.

"I see. And your name?"

"Lisbeth. And this is Aleydis." The youngest smiled at me. They were both dressed neatly in brown dresses with white aprons and caps.

"And your older sister?"

"Maertge. Never call her Maria. Our grandmother's name is Maria. Maria Thins. This is her house."

The baby began to whimper. Lisbeth joggled him up and down on her knee.

I looked up at the house. It was certainly grander than ours, but not as grand as I had feared. It had two stories, plus an attic, whereas ours had only the one, with a tiny attic. It was an end house, with the Molenpoort running down one side, so that it was a little wider than the other houses in the street. It felt less pressed in than many of the houses in Delft, which were packed together in narrow rows of brick along the canals, their chimneys and stepped roofs reflected in the green canal water. The ground-floor windows of this house were very high, and on the first floor there

18

were three windows set close together rather than the two of other houses along the street.

From the front of the house the New Church tower was visible just across the canal. A strange view for a Catholic family, I thought. A church they will never even go inside.

"So you're the maid, are you?" I heard behind me.

The woman standing in the doorway had a broad face, pockmarked from an earlier illness. Her nose was bulbous and irregular, and her thick lips were pushed together to form a small mouth. Her eyes were light blue, as if she had caught the sky in them. She wore a grey-brown dress with a white chemise, a cap tied tight around her head, and an apron that was not as clean as mine. She stood blocking the doorway, so that Maertge and Cornelia had to push their way out round her, and looked at me with crossed arms as if waiting for a challenge.

Already she feels threatened by me, I thought. She will bully me if I let her.

"My name is Griet," I said, gazing at her levelly. "I am the new maid."

The woman shifted from one hip to the other. "You'd best come in, then," she said after a moment. She moved back into the shadowy interior so that the doorway was clear.

I stepped across the threshold.

What I always remembered about being in the front hall for the first time were the paintings. I stopped inside the door, clutching my

19

bundle, and stared. I had seen paintings before, but never so many in one room. I counted eleven. The largest painting was of two men, almost naked, wrestling each other. I did not recognize it as a story from the Bible, and wondered if it was a Catholic subject. Other paintings were of more familiar things—piles of fruit, landscapes, ships on the sea, portraits. They seemed to be by several painters. I wondered which of them were my new master's. None was what I had expected of him.

Later I discovered they were all by other painters—he rarely kept his own finished paintings in the house. He was an art dealer as well as an artist, and paintings hung in almost every room, even where I slept. There were more than fifty in all, though the number varied over time as he traded and sold them.

"Come now, no need to idle and gape." The woman hurried down a lengthy hallway, which ran along one side of the house all the way to the back. I followed as she turned abruptly into a room on the left. On the wall directly opposite hung a painting that was larger than me. It was of Christ on the cross, surrounded by the Virgin Mary, Mary Magdalene, and St. John. I tried not to stare but I was amazed by its size and subject. "Catholics are not so different from us," my father had said. But we did not have such pictures in our houses, or our churches, or anywhere. Now I would see this painting every day.

I was always to think of that room as the Crucifixion room. I was never comfortable in it.

The painting surprised me so much that I did not notice the woman in the corner until she spoke. "Well, girl," she said, "that is something new for you to see." She sat in a comfortable chair, smoking a pipe. Her teeth gripping the stem had gone brown, and her fingers were stained with ink. The rest of her was spotless—her black dress, lace collar, stiff white cap. Though her lined face was stern her light brown eyes seemed amused.

She was the kind of old woman who looked as if she would outlive everyone.

She is Catharina's mother, I thought suddenly. It was not just the color of her eyes and the wisp of grey curl that escaped her cap in the same way as her daughter's. She had the manner of someone used to looking after those less able than she—of looking after Catharina. I understood now why I had been brought to her rather than her daughter.

Though she seemed to look at me casually, her gaze was watchful. When she narrowed her eyes I realized she knew everything I was thinking. I turned my head so that my cap hid my face.

Maria Thins puffed on her pipe and chuckled. "That's right, girl. You keep your thoughts to yourself here. So, you're to work for my daughter. She's out now, at the shops. Tanneke here will show you round and explain your duties."

I nodded. "Yes, madam."

Tanneke, who had been standing at the

21

old woman's side, pushed past me. I followed, Maria Thins' eyes branding my back. I heard her chuckling again.

Tanneke took me first to the back of the house, where there were cooking and washing kitchens and two storage rooms. The washing kitchen led out to a tiny courtyard full of drying white laundry.

"This needs ironing, for a start," Tanneke said. I said nothing, though it looked as if the laundry had not yet been bleached properly by the midday sun.

She led me back inside and pointed to a hole in the floor of one of the storage rooms, a ladder leading down into it. "You're to sleep there," she announced. "Drop your things there now and you can sort yourself out later."

I reluctantly let my bundle drop into the dim hole, thinking of the stones Agnes and Frans and I had thrown into the canal to seek out the monsters. My things thudded onto the dirt floor. I felt like an apple tree losing its fruit.

I followed Tanneke back along the hallway, which all the rooms opened off—many more rooms than in our house. Next to the Crucifixion room where Maria Thins sat, towards the front of the house, was a smaller room with children's beds, chamberpots, small chairs and a table, on it various earthenware, candlesticks, snuffers, and clothing, all in a jumble.

"The girls sleep here," Tanneke mumbled, perhaps embarrassed by the mess.

She turned up the hallway again and opened a door into a large room, where light streamed in from the front windows and across the red and grey tiled floor. "The great hall," she muttered. "Master and mistress sleep here."

Their bed was hung with green silk curtains. There was other furniture in the room—a large cupboard inlaid with ebony, a whitewood table pushed up to the windows with several Spanish leather chairs arranged around it. But again it was the paintings that struck me. More hung in this room than anywhere else. I counted to nineteen silently. Most were portraits—they appeared to be members of both families. There was also a painting of the Virgin Mary, and one of the three kings worshipping the Christ Child. I gazed at both uneasily.

"Now, upstairs." Tanneke went first up the steep stairs, then put a finger to her lips. I climbed as quietly as I could. At the top I looked around and saw the closed door. Behind it was a silence that I knew was him.

I stood, my eyes fixed on the door, not daring to move in case it opened and he came out.

Tanneke leaned towards me and whispered, "You'll be cleaning in there, which the young mistress will explain to you later. And these rooms"—she pointed to the doors towards the back of the house— "are *my* mistress's rooms. Only I go in there to clean."

We crept downstairs again. When we were back in the washing kitchen Tanneke said, "You're to take on the laundry for the house." She pointed to a great mound of clothes—they had fallen far behind with their washing. I would struggle to catch up. "There's a cistern in the cooking kitchen but you'd best get your water for washing from the canal—it's clean enough in this part of town."

"Tanneke," I said in a low voice, "have you been doing all this yourself? The cooking and cleaning and washing for the house?"

I had chosen the right words. "*And* some of the shopping." Tanneke puffed up with pride at her own industry. "Young mistress does most of it, of course, but she goes off raw meat and fish when she's carrying a child. And that's *often*," she added in a whisper. "You're to go to the Meat Hall and the fish stalls too. That will be another of your duties."

With that she left me to the laundry. Including me, there were ten of us now in the house, one a baby who would dirty more clothes than the rest. I would be laundering every day, my hands chapped and cracked from the soap and water, my face red from standing over the steam, my back aching from lifting wet cloth, my arms burned by the iron. But I was new and I was young—it was to be expected I would have the hardest tasks.

The laundry needed to soak for a day before I could wash it. In the storage room that led down to the cellar I found two pewter water-pots and a copper kettle. I took the pots with me and walked up the long hallway to the front door.

The girls were sitting on the bench. Now Lisbeth had the bubble blower while Maertge fed

24

baby Johannes bread softened with milk. Cornelia and Aleydis were chasing bubbles. When I appeared they all stopped what they were doing and looked at me expectantly.

"You're the new maid," the girl with the bright red hair declared.

"Yes, Cornelia."

Cornelia picked up a pebble and threw it across the road into the canal. There were long scratches up and down her arm—she must have been bothering the house cat.

"Where will you sleep?" Maertge asked, wiping mushy fingers on her apron.

"In the cellar."

"We like it down there," Cornelia said. "Let's go and play there now!"

She darted inside but did not go far. When no one followed her she came back out, her face cross.

"Aleydis," I said, extending my hand to the youngest girl, "will you show me where to get water from the canal?"

She took my hand and looked up at me. Her eyes were like two shiny grey coins. We crossed the street, Cornelia and Lisbeth following. Aleydis led me to stairs that descended to the water. As we peeked over I tightened my grip on her hand, as I had done years before with Frans and Agnes whenever we stood next to water.

"You stand back from the edge," I ordered. Aleydis obediently took a step back. But Cornelia followed close behind me as I carried the pots down the steps.

"Cornelia, are you going to help me carry the water? If not, go back up to your sisters."

She looked at me, and then she did the worst thing. If she had sulked or shouted, I would know I had mastered her. Instead she laughed.

I reached over and slapped her. Her face turned red, but she did not cry. She ran back up the steps. Aleydis and Lisbeth peered down at me solemnly.

I had a feeling then. This is how it will be with her mother, I thought, except that I will not be able to slap her.

I filled the pots and carried them to the top of the steps. Cornelia had disappeared. Maertge was still sitting with Johannes. I took one of the pots inside and back to the cooking kitchen, where I built up the fire, filled the copper kettle, and put it on to heat.

When I came back Cornelia was outside again, her face still flushed. The girls were playing with tops on the grey and white tiles. None of them looked up at me.

The pot I had left was missing. I looked into the canal and saw it floating, upside down, just out of reach of the stairs.

"Yes, you will be a handful," I murmured. I looked around for a stick to fish it out with but could find none. I filled the other pot again and carried it inside, turning my head so that the girls could not see my face. I set the pot next to the kettle on the fire. Then I went outside again, this time with a broom.

26

Cornelia was throwing stones at the pot, probably hoping to sink it.

"I'll slap you again if you don't stop."

"I'll tell our mother. Maids don't slap us." Cornelia threw another stone.

"Shall I tell your grandmother what you've done?"

A fearful look crossed Cornelia's face. She dropped the stones she held.

A boat was moving along the canal from the direction of the Town Hall. I recognized the man poling from earlier that day—he had delivered his load of bricks and the boat was riding much higher. He grinned when he saw me.

I blushed. "Please, sir," I began, "can you help me get that pot?"

"Oh, you're looking at me now that you want something from me, are you? There's a change!"

Cornelia was watching me curiously.

I swallowed. "I can't reach the pot from here. Perhaps you could—"

The man leaned over, fished out the pot, dumped the water from it, and held it out to me. I ran down the steps and took it from him. "Thank you. I'm most grateful."

He did not let go of the pot. "Is that all I get? No kiss?" He reached over and pulled my sleeve. I jerked my arm away and wrestled the pot from him.

"Not this time," I said as lightly as I could. I was never good at that sort of talk.

He laughed. "I'll be looking for pots every

time I pass here now, won't I, young miss?"
He winked at Cornelia. "Pots and kisses." He
took up his pole and pushed off.

As I climbed the steps back to the street I
thought I saw a movement in the middle
window on the first floor, the room where
he was. I stared but could see nothing except
the reflected sky.

Catharina returned while I was taking down
laundry in the courtyard. I first heard her
keys jangling in the hallway. They hung in a
great bunch just below her waist, bouncing
against her hip. Although they looked uncomfortable to me, she wore them with great
pride. I then heard her in the cooking kitchen,
giving orders to Tanneke and the boy who had
carried things from the shops for her. She
spoke harshly to both.

I continued to pull down and fold bed-
sheets, napkins, pillowcases, tablecloths,
shirts, chemises, aprons, handkerchiefs, collars, caps. They had been hung carelessly,
bunched in places so that patches of cloth were
still damp. And they had not been shaken
first, so there were creases everywhere. I
would be ironing much of the day to make them
presentable.

Catharina appeared at the door, looking
hot and tired, though the sun was not yet at
its highest. Her chemise puffed out messily from
the top of her blue dress, and the green house-

coat she wore over it was already crumpled. Her blond hair was frizzier than ever, especially as she wore no cap to smooth it. The curls fought against the combs that held them in a bun.

She looked as if she needed to sit quietly for a moment by the canal, where the sight of the water might calm and cool her.

I was not sure how I should be with her— I had never been a maid, nor had we ever had one in our house. There were no servants on our street. No one could afford one. I placed the laundry I was folding in a basket, then nodded at her. "Good morning, madam."

She frowned and I realized I should have let her speak first. I would have to take more care with her.

"Tanneke has taken you round the house?" she said.

"Yes, madam."

"Well, then, you will know what to do and you will do it." She hesitated, as if at a loss for words, and it came to me that she knew little more about being my mistress than I did about being her maid. Tanneke had probably been trained by Maria Thins and still followed her orders, whatever Catharina said to her.

I would have to help her without seeming to.

"Tanneke has explained that besides the laundry you want me to go for the meat and fish, madam," I suggested gently.

Catharina brightened. "Yes. She will take

29

you when you finish with the washing here. After that you will go every day yourself. And on other errands as I need you," she added.

"Yes, madam." I waited. When she said nothing else I reached up to pull a man's linen shirt from the line.

Catharina stared at the shirt. "Tomorrow," she announced as I was folding it, "I will show you upstairs where you are to clean. Early—first thing in the morning." Before I could reply she disappeared inside.

After I brought in the laundry I found the iron, cleaned it, and set it in the fire to heat. I had just begun ironing when Tanneke came and handed me a shopping pail. "We're going to the butcher's now," she said. "I'll need the meat soon." I had heard her clattering in the cooking kitchen and had smelled parsnips roasting.

Out in front Catharina sat on the bench, with Lisbeth on a stool by her feet and Johannes asleep in a cradle. She was combing Lisbeth's hair and searching for lice. Next to her Cornelia and Aleydis were sewing. "No, Aleydis," Catharina was saying, "pull the thread tight, that's too loose. You show her, Cornelia."

I had not thought they could all be so calm together.

Maertge ran over from the canal. "Are you going to the butcher's? May I go too, Mama?"

"Only if you stay with Tanneke and mind her."

I was glad that Maertge came with us. Tanneke was still wary of me, but Maertge was merry and quick and that made it easier for us to be friendly.

I asked Tanneke how long she had worked for Maria Thins.

"Oh, many years," she said. "A few before master and young mistress were married and came to live here. I started when I was no older than you. How old are you, then?"

"Sixteen."

"I began when I was fourteen," Tanneke countered triumphantly. "Half my life I've worked here."

I would not have said such a thing with pride. Her work had worn her so that she looked older than her twenty-eight years.

The Meat Hall was just behind the Town Hall, south and to the west of Market Square. Inside were thirty-two stalls—there had been thirty-two butchers in Delft for generations. It was busy with housewives and maids choosing, bartering and buying for their families, and men carrying carcasses back and forth. Sawdust on the floor soaked up blood and clung to shoes and hems of dresses. There was a tang of blood in the air that always made me shiver, though at one time I had gone there every week and ought to have grown used to the smell. Still, I was pleased to be in a familiar place. As we passed between the stalls the butcher we used to buy our meat from before my father's accident called out to me. I smiled at him, relieved to see a face I knew. It was the first time I had smiled all day.

It was strange to meet so many new people

and see so many new things in one morning, and to do so apart from all the familiar things that made up my life. Before, if I met someone new I was always surrounded by family and neighbors. If I went to a new place I was with Frans or my mother or father and felt no threat. The new was woven in with the old, like the darning in a sock.

Frans told me not long after he began his apprenticeship that he had almost run away, not from the hard work, but because he could not face the strangeness day after day. What kept him there was knowing that our father had spent all his savings on the apprentice fee, and would have sent him right back if he had come home. Besides, he would find much more strangeness out in the world if he went elsewhere.

"I will come and see you," I whispered to the butcher, "when I am alone." Then I hurried to catch up with Tanneke and Maertge.

They had stopped at a stall farther along. The butcher there was a handsome man, with graying blond curls and bright blue eyes.

"Pieter, this is Griet," Tanneke said. "She will be fetching the meat for us now. You're to add it to our account as usual."

I tried to keep my eyes on his face, but I could not help glancing down at his blood-splattered apron. Our butcher always wore a clean apron when he was selling, changing it whenever he got blood on it.

"Ah." Pieter looked me over as if I were a plump chicken he was considering roasting. "What would you like today, Griet?"

I turned to Tanneke. "Four pounds of chops and a pound of tongue," she ordered.

Pieter smiled. "And what do you think of that, miss?" he addressed Maertge. "Don't I sell the best tongue in Delft?"

Maertge nodded and giggled as she gazed at the display of joints, chops, tongue, pigs' feet, sausages.

"You'll find, Griet, that I have the best meat and the most honest scales in the hall," Pieter remarked as he weighed the tongue. "You'll have no complaints about me."

I stared at his apron and swallowed. Pieter put the chops and tongue into the pail I carried, winked at me and turned to serve the next customer.

We went next to the fish stalls, just beside the Meat Hall. Seagulls hovered above the stalls, waiting for the fishheads and innards the fishmongers threw into the canal. Tanneke introduced me to their fishmonger—also different from ours. I was to alternate each day between meat and fish.

When we left I did not want to go back to the house, to Catharina and the children on the bench. I wanted to walk home. I wanted to step into my mother's kitchen and hand her the pailful of chops. We had not eaten meat in months.

Catharina was combing through Cornelia's hair when we returned. They paid no attention to me. I helped Tanneke with dinner, turning the meat on the grill, fetching things for the table in the great hall, cutting the bread.

When the meal was ready the girls came in, Maertge joining Tanneke in the cooking kitchen while the others sat down in the great hall. I had just placed the tongue in the meat barrel in one of the storage rooms—Tanneke had left it out and the cat had almost got to it—when he appeared from outside, standing in the doorway at the end of the long hall, wearing his hat and cloak. I stood still and he paused, the light behind him so that I could not see his face. I did not know if he was looking down the hallway at me. After a moment he disappeared into the great hall.

Tanneke and Maertge served while I looked after the baby in the Crucifixion room. When Tanneke was done she joined me and we ate and drank what the family did—chops, parsnips, bread, and mugs of beer. Although Pieter's meat was no better than our family butcher's, it was a welcome taste after going so long without. The bread was rye rather than the cheaper brown bread we had been eating, and the beer was not so watery either.

I did not wait on the family at that dinner and so I did not see him. Occasionally I heard his voice, usually along with Maria Thins'. From their tones it was clear they got on well.

After dinner Tanneke and I cleared up, then mopped the floors of the kitchens and storage rooms. The walls of each kitchen were tiled in white, and the fireplace in blue and white Delft tiles painted with birds in one section, ships in another, and soldiers in another. I studied them carefully, but none had been painted by my father.

I spent most of the rest of the day ironing in the washing kitchen, occasionally stopping to build up the fire, fetch wood, or step into the courtyard to escape the heat. The girls played in and out of the house, sometimes coming in to watch me and poke at the fire, another time to tease Tanneke when they found her asleep next door in the cooking kitchen, Johannes crawling around her feet. They were a little uneasy with me—perhaps they thought I might slap them. Cornelia scowled at me and did not stay long in the room, but Maertge and Lisbeth took the clothes I had ironed and put them away for me in the cupboard in the great hall. Their mother was asleep there. "The last month before the baby comes she'll stay in bed much of the day," Tanneke confided, "propped up with pillows all around her."

Maria Thins had gone to her upstairs rooms after dinner. Once, though, I heard her in the hallway and when I looked up she was standing in the doorway, watching me. She said nothing, so I turned back to my ironing and pretended she wasn't there. After a moment out of the corner of my eye I saw her nod and shuffle off.

He had a guest upstairs—I heard two male voices as they climbed up. Later when I heard them coming down I peeked around the door to watch them go out. The man with him was plump and wore a long white feather in his hat.

When it got dark we lit candles, and Tanneke and I had bread and cheese and beer with the children in the Crucifixion room while the others ate tongue in the great hall. I was careful to sit with my back to the Crucifixion scene. I was so exhausted I could hardly think. At home I had worked just as hard but it was never so tiring as in a strange house where everything was new and I was always tense and serious. At home I had been able to laugh with my mother or Agnes or Frans. Here there was no one to laugh with.

I had not yet been down to the cellar where I was to sleep. I took a candle with me but was too tired to look around beyond finding a bed, pillow and blanket. Leaving the trap door of the cellar open so that cool, fresh air could reach me, I took off my shoes, cap, apron and dress, prayed briefly, and lay down. I was about to blow out the candle when I noticed the painting hanging at the foot of my bed. I sat up, wide awake now. It was another picture of Christ on the Cross, smaller than the one upstairs but even more disturbing. Christ had thrown his head back in pain, and Mary Magdalene's eyes were rolling. I lay back gingerly, unable to take my eyes off it. I could not imagine sleeping in the room with the painting. I wanted to take it down but did not dare. Finally I blew out the candle—I could not afford to waste candles on my first day in the new house. I lay back again, my eyes fixed to the place where I knew the painting hung.

I slept badly that night, tired as I was. I woke often and looked for the painting. Though I could see nothing on the wall, every detail was fixed in my mind. Finally, when it was beginning to grow light, the painting appeared again and I was sure the Virgin Mary was looking down at me.

When I got up in the morning I tried not to look at the painting, instead studying the contents of the cellar in the dim light that fell through the window in the storage room above me. There was not much to see—several tapestry-covered chairs piled up, a few other broken chairs, a mirror, and two more paintings, both still lifes, leaning against the wall. Would anyone notice if I replaced the Crucifixion with a still life?

Cornelia would. And she would tell her mother.

I did not know what Catharina—or any of them—thought of my being Protestant. It was a curious feeling, having to be aware of it myself. I had never before been outnumbered.

I turned my back on the painting and climbed the ladder. Catharina's keys were clinking at the front of the house and I went to find her. She moved slowly, as if she were half asleep, but she made an effort to draw herself up when she saw me. She led me up the stairs, climbing slowly, holding tightly to the rail to pull her bulk up.

At the studio she searched among the keys, then unlocked and pushed open the door. The room was dark, the shutters closed—I could make out only a little from the cracks of light streaming in between them. The room gave off a clean, sharp odor of linseed oil that reminded me of my father's clothes when he had returned from the tile factory at night. It smelled like wood and fresh-cut hay mixed together.

Catharina remained on the threshold. I did not dare enter before her. After an awkward moment she ordered, "Open the shutters, then. Not the window on the left. Just the middle and far windows. And only the lower part of the middle window."

I crossed the room, edging around an easel and chair to the middle window. I pulled open the lower window, then opened out the shutters. I did not look at the painting on the easel, not while Catharina was watching me from the doorway.

A table had been pushed up against the window on the right, with a chair set in the corner. The chair's back and seat were of leather tooled with yellow flowers and leaves.

"Don't move anything over there," Catharina reminded me. "That is what he is painting."

Even if I stood on my toes I was too small to reach the upper window and shutters. I would have to stand on the chair, but did not want to do so in front of her. She made me nervous, waiting in the doorway for me to make a mistake.

I considered what to do.

It was the baby who saved me—he began wailing downstairs. Catharina shifted from one hip to the other. As I hesitated she grew impatient and finally left to tend to Johannes.

I quickly climbed up and stood carefully on the wooden frame of the chair, pulled open the upper window, leaned out and pushed the shutters open. Peeking down at the street below, I spied Tanneke scrubbing the tiles in front of the house. She did not see me, but a cat padding across the wet tiles behind her paused and looked up.

I opened the lower window and shutters and got down from the chair. Something moved in front of me and I froze. The movement stopped. It was me, reflected in a mirror that hung on the wall between the two windows. I gazed at myself. Although I had an anxious, guilty expression, my face was also bathed in light, making my skin glow. I stared, surprised, then stepped away.

Now that I had a moment I surveyed the room. It was a large, square space, not as long as the great hall downstairs. With the windows open it was bright and airy, with whitewashed walls, and grey and white marble tiles on the floor, the darker tiles set in a pattern of square crosses. A row of Delft tiles painted with cupids lined the bottom of the walls to protect the whitewash from our mops. They were not my father's.

Though it was a big room, it held little furniture. There was the easel and chair set in front of the middle window, and the table placed in front of the window in the right corner. Besides the chair I had stood on there was another by the table, of plain leather nailed on with brass studs and two lion heads carved into the tops of the posts. Against the far wall, behind the chair and easel, was a small cupboard, its drawers closed, several brushes and a knife with a diamond-shaped blade arranged on top next to clean palettes. Beside the cupboard was a desk on which were papers and books and prints. Two more lion-head chairs had been set against the wall near the doorway.

It was an orderly room, empty of the clutter of everyday life. It felt different from the rest of the house, almost as if it were in another house altogether. When the door was closed it would be difficult to hear the shouts of the children, the jangle of Catharina's keys, the sweeping of our brooms.

I took up my broom, bucket of water, and dustcloth and began to clean. I started in the corner where the scene of the painting had been set up, where I knew I must not move a thing. I kneeled on the chair to dust the window I had struggled to open, and the yellow curtain that hung to one side of it in the corner, touching it lightly so that I would not disturb its folds. The panes of glass were dirty and needed scrubbing with warm water, but I was not sure if he wanted them clean. I would have to ask Catharina.

I dusted the chairs, polishing the brass studs and lion heads. The table had not been cleaned properly in some time. Someone had wiped around the objects placed there—a powder-brush, a pewter bowl, a letter, a black ceramic pot, blue cloth heaped to one side and hanging over the edge—but they had to be moved for the table really to be cleaned. As my mother had said, I would have to find a way to move things yet put them back exactly as if they had not been touched.

The letter lay close to the corner of the table. If I placed my thumb along one edge of the paper, my second finger along another, and anchored my hand with my smallest finger hooked to the table edge, I should be able to move the letter, dust there, and replace it where my hand indicated.

I laid my fingers against the edges and drew in my breath, then removed the letter, dusted, and replaced it all in one quick movement. I was not sure why I felt I had to do it quickly. I stood back from the table. The letter seemed to be in the right place, though only he would really know.

Still, if this was to be my test, I had best get it done.

From the letter I measured with my hand to the powder-brush, then placed my fingers at various points around one side of the brush. I removed it, dusted, replaced it, and measured the space between it and the letter. I did the same with the bowl.

This was how I cleaned without seeming to

41

move anything. I measured each thing in relation to the objects around it and the space between them. The small things on the table were easy, the furniture harder—I used my feet, my knees, sometimes my shoulders and chin with the chairs.

I did not know what to do with the blue cloth heaped messily on the table. I would not be able to get the folds exact if I moved the cloth. For now I left it alone, hoping that for a day or two he would not notice until I had found a way to clean it.

With the rest of the room I could be less careful. I dusted and swept and mopped—the floor, the walls, the windows, the furniture—with the satisfaction of tackling a room in need of a good cleaning. In the far corner, opposite the table and window, a door led to a storeroom, filled with paintings and canvases, chairs, chests, dishes, bedpans, a coat rack and a row of books. I cleaned in there too, tidying the things away so that there was more order to the room.

All the while I had avoided cleaning around the easel. I did not know why, but I was nervous about seeing the painting that sat on it. At last, though, there was nothing left to do. I dusted the chair in front of the easel, then began to dust the easel itself, trying not to look at the painting.

When I glimpsed the yellow satin, however, I had to stop.

I was still staring at the painting when Maria Thins spoke.

"Not a common sight, now, is it?"

I had not heard her come in. She stood inside the doorway, slightly stooped, wearing a fine black dress and lace collar.

I did not know what to say, and I couldn't help it—I turned back to the painting.

Maria Thins laughed. "You're not the only one to forget your manners in front of one of his paintings, girl." She came over to stand beside me. "Yes, he's managed this one well. That's van Ruijven's wife." I recognized the name as the patron my father had mentioned. "She's not beautiful but he makes her so," she added. "It will fetch a good price."

Because it was the first painting of his I was to see, I always remembered it better than the others, even those I saw grow from the first layer of underpaint to the final highlights.

A woman stood in front of a table, turned towards a mirror on the wall so that she was in profile. She wore a mantle of rich yellow satin trimmed with white ermine, and a fashionable five-pointed red ribbon in her hair. A window lit her from the left, falling across her face and tracing the delicate curve of her forehead and nose. She was tying a string of pearls around her neck, holding the ribbons up, her hands suspended in the air. Entranced with herself in the mirror, she did not seem to be aware that anyone was looking at her. Behind her on a bright white wall was an old map, in the dark foreground the table with the letter on it, the powder-brush and the other things I had dusted around.

I wanted to wear the mantle and the pearls. I wanted to know the man who painted her like that.

I thought of me looking at my reflection in the mirror earlier and was ashamed.

Maria Thins seemed content to stand with me and contemplate the painting. It was odd to look at it with the setting just behind it. Already from my dusting I knew all of the objects on the table, and their relation to one another—the letter by the corner, the powder-brush lying casually next to the pewter bowl, the blue cloth bunched around the dark pot. Everything seemed to be exactly the same, except cleaner and purer. It made a mockery of my own cleaning.

Then I saw a difference. I drew in my breath.

"What is it, girl?"

"In the painting there are no lion heads on the chair next to the woman," I said.

"No. There was once a lute sitting on that chair as well. He makes plenty of changes. He doesn't paint just what he sees, but what will suit. Tell me, girl, do you think this painting is done?"

I stared at her. Her question must be a trick but I could not imagine any change that would make it better.

"Isn't it?" I faltered.

Maria Thins snorted. "He's been working on it for three months. I expect he'll do so for two more months. He will change things. You'll see." She looked around. "Done your

cleaning, have you? Well, then, go on, girl—
go to your other tasks. He'll come soon to see
how you've done."

I looked at the painting one last time, but
by studying it so hard I felt something slip away.
It was like looking at a star in the night sky—
if I looked at one directly I could barely see
it, but if I looked from the corner of my eye
it became much brighter.

I gathered my broom and bucket and cloth.
When I left the room, Maria Thins was still
standing in front of the painting.

I filled the pots from the canal and set them
on the fire, then went to find Tanneke. She
was in the room where the girls slept, helping
Cornelia to dress while Maertge helped
Aleydis and Lisbeth helped herself. Tanneke was not in good spirits, glancing at me
only to ignore me as I tried to speak to her.
Finally I stood directly in front of her so
that she had to look at me. "Tanneke, I'll go
to the fish stalls now. What would you like
today?"

"Going so early? We always go later in the
day." Tanneke still did not look at me. She was
tying white ribbons into five-pointed stars
in Cornelia's hair.

"I'm free while the water is heating and
thought I would go now," I replied simply. I
did not add that the best cuts were to be had
early, even if the butcher or fishmonger

promised to set aside things for the family. She should know that. "What would you like?"

"Don't fancy fish today. Go to the butcher's for a mutton joint." Tanneke finished with the ribbons and Cornelia jumped up and pushed past me. Tanneke turned away and opened a chest to search for something. I watched her broad back for a moment, the greyish brown dress pulled tight across it.

She was jealous of me. I had cleaned the studio, where she was not allowed, where no one, it seemed, could go except me and Maria Thins.

When Tanneke straightened, a bonnet in her hand, she said, "The master painted me once, you know. Painted me pouring milk. Everyone said it was his best painting."

"I'd like to see it," I responded. "Is it still here?"

"Oh no, van Ruijven bought it."

I thought for a moment. "So one of Delft's wealthiest men takes pleasure in looking at you each day."

Tanneke grinned, her pocked face growing even wider. The right words changed her mood in a moment. It was simply up to me to find the words.

I turned to go before her mood could sour. "May I come with you?" Maertge asked.

"And me?" Lisbeth added.

"Not today," I said firmly. "You have something to eat and help Tanneke." I did not want it to become habit for the girls to accompany me. I would use it as a reward for minding me.

I was also longing to walk in familiar streets on my own, not to have a constant reminder of my new life chattering at my side. As I stepped into Market Square, leaving Papists' Corner behind, I breathed in deeply. I had not realized that I had been holding myself in tight all the time I was with the family.

Before going to Pieter's stall I stopped at the butcher I knew, who beamed when he saw me. "At last you decide to say hello! What, yesterday you were too grand for the likes of me?" he teased.

I started to explain my new situation but he interrupted me. "Of course I know. Everyone is talking—Jan the tiler's daughter has gone to work for the painter Vermeer. And then I see after one day she is already too proud to speak to old friends!"

"I have nothing to be so proud of, becoming a maid. My father is ashamed."

"Your father was simply unlucky. No one is blaming him. There is no need for you to be ashamed, my dear. Except of course that you are not buying your meat from me."

"I have no choice, I'm afraid. That's for my mistress to decide."

"Oh, it is, is it? So your buying from Pieter has nothing to do with his handsome son?"

I frowned. "I have not seen his son."

The butcher laughed. "You will, you will. Off you go. When you see your mother next tell her to come and see me. I will set aside something for her."

I thanked him and passed along the stalls

to Pieter's. He seemed surprised to see me. "Here already, are you? Couldn't wait to get here for more of that tongue?"

"I'd like a joint of mutton today, please."

"Now tell me, Griet, was that not the best tongue you have had?"

I refused to give him the compliment he craved. "The master and mistress ate it. They did not remark on it."

Behind Pieter a young man turned round— he had been cutting into a side of beef at a table behind the stall. He must have been the son, for though he was taller than his father, he had the same bright blue eyes. His blond hair was long and thick with curls, framing a face that made me think of apricots. Only his bloody apron was displeasing to the eye.

His eyes came to rest on me like a butterfly on a flower and I could not keep from blushing. I repeated my request for mutton, keeping my eyes on his father. Pieter rummaged through his meat and pulled out a joint for me, laying it on the counter. Two sets of eyes watched me.

The joint was grey at the edges. I sniffed the meat. "This is not fresh," I said bluntly. "Mistress will be none too pleased that you expect her family to eat meat such as this." My tone was haughtier than I had intended. Perhaps it needed to be.

Father and son stared at me. I held the gaze of the father, trying to ignore the son.

At last Pieter turned to his son. "Pieter, get me that joint set aside on the cart."

"But that's meant for—" Pieter the son stopped. He disappeared, returning with another joint, which I could immediately see was superior. I nodded. "That's better."

Pieter the son wrapped the joint and placed it in my pail. I thanked him. As I turned to go I caught the glance that passed between father and son. Even then I knew somehow what it meant, and what it would mean for me.

Catharina was sitting on the bench when I got back, feeding Johannes. I showed her the joint and she nodded. As I was about to go in she said in a low voice, "My husband has inspected the studio and found the cleaning suited him." She did not look at me.

"Thank you, madam." I stepped inside, glanced at a still life of fruits and a lobster, and thought, So, I really am to stay.

The rest of the day passed much as the first had, and as the days to follow would. Once I had cleaned the studio and gone to the fish stalls or the Meat Hall I began again on the laundry, one day sorting, soaking and working on stains, another day scrubbing, rinsing, boiling and wringing before hanging things to dry and be bleached in the noon sun, another day ironing and mending and folding. At some point I always stopped to help Tanneke with the midday meal. Afterwards we cleaned up, and then I had a little time free to rest and sew on the bench out front, or back in the courtyard. After that I finished whatever I had been doing in the morning, then helped Tanneke with the late meal. The last thing we did was to mop the floors once more so that they would be fresh and clean for the morning.

At night I covered the Crucifixion hanging at the foot of my bed with the apron I had worn that day. I slept better then. The next day I added the apron to the day's wash.

While Catharina was unlocking the studio door on the second morning I asked her if I should clean the windows.

"Why not?" she answered sharply. "You do not need to ask me such petty things."

"Because of the light, madam," I explained. "It might change the painting if I clean them. You see?"

She did not see. She would not or could not come into the room to look at the painting. It seemed she never entered the studio. When Tanneke was in the right mood I would have to ask her why. Catharina went downstairs to ask him and called up to me to leave the windows.

When I cleaned the studio I saw nothing to indicate that he had been there at all. Nothing had been moved, the palettes were clean, the painting itself appeared no different. But I could feel that he had been there.

I had seen very little of him the first two days

I was in the house on the Oude Langendijck. I heard him sometimes, on the stairs, in the hallway, chuckling with his children, talking softly to Catharina. Hearing his voice made me feel as if I were walking along the edge of a canal and unsure of my steps. I did not know how he would treat me in his own house, whether or not he would pay attention to the vegetables I chopped in his kitchen.

No gentleman had ever taken such an interest in me before.

I came face to face with him my third day in the house. Just before dinner I went to find a plate that Lisbeth had left outside and almost ran into him as he carried Aleydis in his arms down the hallway.

I stepped back. He and Aleydis regarded me with the same grey eyes. He neither smiled nor did not smile at me. It was hard to meet his eyes. I thought of the woman looking at herself in the painting upstairs, of wearing pearls and yellow satin. She would have no trouble meeting the gaze of a gentleman. When I managed to lift my eyes to his he was no longer looking at me.

The next day I saw the woman herself. On my way back from the butcher a man and woman walked ahead of me on the Oude Langendijck. At our door he turned to her and bowed, then walked on. There was a long white feather in his hat—he must have been the visitor from a few days earlier. From the brief glimpse I caught of his profile I saw that he had a moustache, and a plump face to match his body. He smiled as if he were about to pay a flattering but false compliment. The woman turned into the house before I could see her face but I did see the five-pointed red ribbon in her hair. I held back, waiting by the doorway until I heard her go up the stairs.

Later I was putting away some clothes in the cupboard in the great hall when she came back down. I stood up as she entered. She was carrying the yellow mantle in her arms. The ribbon was still in her hair.

"Oh!" she said. "Where is Catharina?"

"She's gone with her mother to the Town Hall, madam. Family business."

"I see. Never mind, I'll see her another day. I'll leave this here for her." She draped the mantle across the bed and dropped the pearl necklace on top of it.

"Yes, madam."

I could not take my eyes off her. I felt as if I were seeing her and yet not seeing her. It was a strange sensation. She was, as Maria Thins had said, not as beautiful as when the light struck her in the painting. Yet she was beautiful, if only because I was remembering her so. She gazed at me with a puzzled look on her face, as if she ought to know me since I was staring at her with such familiarity. I managed to lower my eyes. "I will tell her you called, madam."

She nodded but looked troubled. She glanced at the pearls she had laid on top of the mantle. "I think I shall leave these up in the studio with him," she announced, picking up the necklace.

She did not look at me, but I knew she was thinking that maids were not to be trusted with pearls. After she had gone her face lingered like perfume.

On Saturday Catharina and Maria Thins took Tanneke and Maertge with them to the market in the square, where they would buy vegetables to last the week, staples and other things for the house. I longed to go with them, thinking I might see my mother and sister, but I was told to stay at the house with the younger girls and the baby. It was difficult to keep them from running off to the market. I would have taken them there myself but I did not dare leave the house unattended. Instead we watched the boats go up and down the canal, full on their way to the market with cabbages, pigs, flowers, wood, flour, strawberries, horseshoes. They were empty on the way back, the boatmen counting money or drinking. I taught the girls games I had played with Agnes and Frans, and they taught me games they had made up. They blew bubbles, played with their dolls, ran with their hoops while I sat on the bench with Johannes in my lap.

Cornelia seemed to have forgotten about the slap. She was cheerful and friendly, helpful with Johannes, obedient to me. "Will you help me?" she asked me as she tried to climb onto a barrel the neighbors had left out in the street. Her light brown eyes were wide and innocent. I found myself warming to her sweetness, yet knowing I could not trust her. She could be the most interesting of the girls, but also the most changeable—the best and the worst at the same time.

They were sorting through a collection of shells they had brought outside, dividing them into piles of different colors, when he came out of the house. I squeezed the baby round his middle, feeling his ribs under my hands. He squealed and I buried my nose in his ear to hide my face.

"Papa, can I go with you?" Cornelia cried, jumping up and grabbing his hand. I could not see the expression on his face—the tilt of his head and the brim of his hat hid it.

Lisbeth and Aleydis abandoned their shells. "I want to go too!" they shouted in unison, grabbing his other hand.

He shook his head and then I could see his bemused expression. "Not today—I'm going to the apothecary's."

"Will you buy paint things, Papa?" Cornelia asked, still holding on to his hand.

"Among other things."

Baby Johannes began to cry and he glanced down at me. I bounced the baby, feeling awkward.

He looked as if he would say something, but instead he shook off the girls and strode down the Oude Langendijck.

He had not said a word to me since we discussed the color and shape of vegetables.

I woke very early on Sunday, for I was excited to go home. I had to wait for Catharina to unlock the front door, but when I heard it swing open I came out to find Maria Thins with the key.

"My daughter is tired today," she said as she stood aside to let me out. "She will rest for a few days. Can you manage without her?"

"Of course, madam," I replied, then added, "and I may always ask you if I have questions."

Maria Thins chuckled. "Ah, you're a cunning one, girl. You know whose pot to spoon from. Never mind, we can do with a bit of cleverness around here." She handed me some coins, my wages for the days I had worked. "Off you go now, to tell your mother all about us, I suspect."

I slipped away before she could say more, crossed Market Square, past those going to early services at the New Church, and hurried up the streets and canals that led me home. When I turned into my street I thought how different it felt already after less than a week away. The light seemed brighter and flatter, the canal wider. The plane trees lining the canal stood perfectly still, like sentries waiting for me.

Agnes was sitting on the bench in front of the house. When she saw me she called inside, "She's here!" then ran to me and took my arm. "How is it?" she asked, not even saying hello.

"Are they nice? Do you work hard? Are there any girls there? Is the house very grand? Where do you sleep? Do you eat off fine plates?"

I laughed and would not answer any of her questions until I had hugged my mother and greeted my father. Although it was not very much, I felt proud to hand over to my mother the few coins in my hand. This was, after all, why I was working.

My father came to sit outside with us and hear about my new life. I gave my hands to him to guide him over the front stoop. As he sat down on the bench he rubbed my palms with his thumb. "Your hands are chapped," he said. "So rough and worn. Already you have the scars of hard work."

"Don't worry," I answered lightly. "There was so much laundry waiting for me because they didn't have enough help before. It will get easier soon."

My mother studied my hands. "I'll soak some bergamot in oil," she said. "That will keep your hands soft. Agnes and I will go into the country to pick some."

"Tell us!" Agnes cried. "Tell us about them."

I told them. Only a few things I didn't mention—how tired I was at night; how the Crucifixion scene hung at the foot of my bed; how I had slapped Cornelia; how Maertge and Agnes were the same age. Otherwise I told them everything.

I passed on the message from our butcher

to my mother. "That is kind of him," she said, "but he knows we have no money for meat and will not take such charity."

"I don't think he meant it as charity," I explained. "I think he meant it out of friendship."

She did not answer, but I knew she would not go back to the butcher.

When I mentioned the new butchers, Pieter the father and son, she raised her eyebrows but said nothing.

Afterwards we went to services at our church, where I was surrounded by familiar faces and familiar words. Sitting between Agnes and my mother, I felt my back relaxing into the pew, and my face softening from the mask I had worn all week. I thought I might cry.

Mother and Agnes would not let me help them with dinner when we came back home. I sat with my father on the bench in the sun. He held his face up to the warmth and kept his head cocked that way all the time we talked.

"Now, Griet," he said, "tell me about your new master. You hardly said a word about him."

"I haven't seen much of him," I replied truthfully. "He is either in his studio, where no one is to disturb him, or he is out."

"Taking care of Guild business, I expect. But you have been in his studio—you told us about the cleaning and the measurements, but nothing about the painting he is working on. Describe it to me."

"I don't know if I can in such a way that you will be able to see it."

"Try. I have little to think of now except for memories. It will give me pleasure to imagine a painting by a master, even if my mind creates only a poor imitation."

So I tried to describe the woman tying pearls around her neck, her hands suspended, gazing at herself in the mirror, the light from the window bathing her face and her yellow mantle, the dark foreground that separated her from us.

My father listened intently, but his own face was not illuminated until I said, "The light on the back wall is so warm that looking at it feels the way the sun feels on your face."

He nodded and smiled, pleased now that he understood.

"This is what you like best about your new life," he said presently. "Being in the studio."

The only thing, I thought, but did not say.

When we ate dinner I tried not to compare it with that in the house at Papists' Corner, but already I had become accustomed to meat and good rye bread. Although my mother was a better cook than Tanneke, the brown bread was dry, the vegetable stew tasteless with no fat to flavor it. The room, too, was different—no marble tiles, no thick silk curtains, no tooled leather chairs. Everything was simple and clean, without ornamentation. I loved it because I knew it, but I was aware now of its dullness.

At the end of the day it was hard saying goodbye to my parents—harder than when I had first left, because this time I knew what I was going back to. Agnes walked with me as far as Market Square. When we were alone, I asked her how she was.

"Lonely," she replied, a sad word from a young girl. She had been lively all day but had now grown subdued.

"I'll come every Sunday," I promised. "And perhaps during the week I can come quickly to say hello after I've gone for the meat or fish."

"Or I can come to see you when you are out buying things," she suggested, brightening.

We did manage to meet in the Meat Hall several times. I was always glad to see her—as long as I was alone.

I began to find my place at the house on the Oude Langendijck. Catharina, Tanneke and Cornelia were all difficult at times, but usually I was left alone to my work. This may have been Maria Thins' influence. She had decided, for her own reasons, that I was a useful addition, and the others, even the children, followed her example.

Perhaps she felt the clothes were cleaner and better bleached now that I had taken on the laundry. Or that the meat was more tender now that I chose it. Or that he was happier with a clean studio. These first two things were true. The last, I did not know. When he and I finally spoke it was not about my cleaning.

I was careful to deflect any praise for better housekeeping from myself. I did not want to make enemies. If Maria Thins liked the meat, I suggested it was Tanneke's cooking that made it so. If Maertge said her apron was whiter than before, I said it was because the summer sun was particularly strong now.

I avoided Catharina when I could. It had been clear from the moment she'd seen me chopping vegetables in my mother's kitchen that she disliked me. Her mood was not improved by the baby she carried, which made her ungainly and nothing like the graceful lady of the house she felt herself to be. It was a hot summer too, and the baby was especially active. It began to kick whenever she walked, or so she said. As she grew bigger she went about the house with a tired, pained look. She took to staying in bed later and later, so that Maria Thins took over her keys and unlocked the studio door for me in the morning. Tanneke and I began to do more and more of her work—looking after the girls, buying things for the house, changing the baby.

One day when Tanneke was in a good mood, I asked her why they did not take on more servants to make things easier. "With a big house like this, and your mistress's wealth, and the master's paintings," I added, "could they not afford another maid? Or a cook?"

"Huh," Tanneke snorted. "They can barely manage to pay you."

I was surprised—the coins amounted to so little in my hand each week. It would take me years of work to be able to buy something as fine as the yellow mantle that Catharina kept so carelessly folded in her cupboard. It did not seem possible that they could be short of money.

"Of course they'll find a way to pay for a nurse for a few months when the baby comes," Tanneke added. She sounded disapproving.

"Why?"

"So she can feed the baby."

"The mistress won't feed her own baby?" I asked stupidly.

"She couldn't have so many children if she fed her own. It stops you having them, you know, if you feed your own."

"Oh." I felt very ignorant of such things. "Does she want more children?"

Tanneke chuckled. "Sometimes I think she's filling the house with children because she can't fill it with servants as she'd like." She lowered her voice. "The master doesn't paint enough to make the money for servants, you see. Three paintings a year he does, usually. Sometimes only two. You don't get rich from that."

"Can he not paint faster?" I knew even as I said it that he would not. He would always paint at his own pace.

"Mistress and young mistress disagree sometimes. Young mistress wants him to paint more, but my mistress says speed would ruin him."

"Maria Thins is very wise." I had learned that I could voice opinions in front of Tanneke as long as Maria Thins was in some way praised. Tanneke was fiercely loyal to her mistress. She had little patience with Catharina, however, and when she was in the right mood she advised me on how to handle her. "Take no notice of what she says," she counseled. "Keep your face empty when she speaks, then do things your own way, or how my mistress or I tell you to do them. She never checks, she never notices. She just orders us about because she feels she has to. But we know who our real mistress is, and so does she."

Although Tanneke was often bad tempered with me, I learned not to take it to heart, as she never remained so for long. She was fickle in her moods, perhaps from being caught between Catharina and Maria Thins for so many years. Despite her confident words about ignoring what Catharina said, Tanneke did not follow her own advice. Catharina's harsh tone upset her. And Maria Thins, for all her fairness, did not defend Tanneke from Catharina. I never once heard Maria Thins berate her daughter for anything, though Catharina needed it at times.

There was also the matter of Tanneke's housekeeping. Perhaps her loyalty made up for her sloppiness about the house—corners unmopped, meat burned on the outside and raw on the inside, pots not scrubbed thoroughly. I could not imagine what she had done to his studio when she tried to clean it. Though Maria Thins rarely scolded Tanneke, they both knew she ought to, and this kept Tanneke uncertain and quick to defend herself.

It became clear to me that in spite of her shrewd ways, Maria Thins was soft on the people closest to her. Her judgment was not as sound as it appeared.

Of the four girls, Cornelia was, as she had shown the first morning, the most unpredictable. Both Lisbeth and Aleydis were good, quiet girls, and Maertge was old enough to begin learning the ways of the house, which steadied her—though occasionally she would have a fit of temper and shout at me much like her mother. Cornelia did not shout, but she was at times ungovernable. Even the threat of Maria Thins' anger that I had used on the first day did not always work. She could be funny and playful one moment, then turn the next, like a purring cat who bites the hand stroking it. While loyal to her sisters, she did not hesitate to make them cry by pinching them hard. I was wary of Cornelia, and could not be fond of her in the way I came to be of the others.

I escaped from them all when I cleaned the studio. Maria Thins unlocked the door for me and sometimes stayed a few minutes to check on the painting, as if it were a sick child she was nursing. Once she left, though, I had the room to myself. I looked around to see if anything had changed. At first it seemed to remain the same, day after day, but after my eyes grew accustomed to the details of the room I began to notice small things—the brushes rearranged on the top of the cupboard, one of the cupboard's drawers left ajar, the palette knife balanced on the easel's ledge, a chair moved a little from its place by the door.

Nothing, however, changed in the corner he was painting. I was careful not to displace any of it, quickly adjusting to my way of measuring so that I was able to clean that area almost as quickly and confidently as the rest of the room. And after experimenting on other bits of cloth, I began to clean the dark blue cloth and yellow curtain with a damp rag, pressing it carefully so that it picked up dust without disturbing the folds.

There seemed to be no changes to the painting, as hard as I looked for them. At last one day I discovered that another pearl had been added to the woman's necklace. Another day the shadow of the yellow curtain had grown bigger. I thought too that some of the fingers on her right hand had been moved.

The satin mantle began to look so real I wanted to reach out and touch it.

I had almost touched the real one the day van Ruijven's wife left it on the bed. I had just been reaching over to stroke the fur collar when I had looked up to see Cornelia in the doorway, watching me. One of the other girls would have asked me what I was doing, but Cornelia had just watched. That was worse than any questions. I had dropped my hand and she'd smiled.

Maertge insisted on coming with me to the fish stalls one morning several weeks after I had begun working at the house. She loved to run through Market Square, looking at things, petting the horses, joining other children in their games, sampling smoked fish from various stalls. She poked me in the ribs as I was buying herring and shouted, "Look, Griet, look at that kite!"

The kite above our heads was shaped like a fish with a long tail, the wind making it look as if it were swimming through the air, with seagulls wheeling around it. As I smiled I saw Agnes hovering near us, her eyes fixed on Maertge. I still had not told Agnes there was a girl her age in the house—I thought it might upset her, that she would feel she was being replaced.

Sometimes when I visited my family at home I felt awkward telling them anything. My new life was taking over the old.

When Agnes looked at me I shook my head slightly so that Maertge would not see, and turned away to put the fish in my pail. I took my time—I could not bear to see the hurt look on her face. I did not know what Maertge would do if Agnes spoke to me.

When I turned around Agnes had gone.

I shall have to explain to her when I see her Sunday, I thought. I have two families now, and they must not mix.

I was always ashamed afterwards that I had turned my back on my own sister.

I was hanging out washing in the courtyard, shaking out each piece before hanging it taut from the line, when Catharina appeared, breathing heavily. She sat down on a chair by the door, closed her eyes and sighed. I continued what I was doing as if it were natural for her to sit with me, but my jaw tightened.

"Are they gone yet?" she asked suddenly.

"Who, madam?"

"Them, you silly girl. My husband and— Go and see if they've gone upstairs yet."

I stepped cautiously into the hallway. Two sets of feet were climbing the stairs.

"Can you manage it?" I heard him say.

"Yes, yes, of course. You know it's not very heavy," another man replied, in a voice deep like a well. "Just a bit cumbersome."

They reached the top of the stairs and entered the studio. I heard the door close.

"Have they gone?" Catharina hissed.

"They are in the studio, madam," I responded.

"Good. Now help me up." Catharina held out her hands and I pulled her to her feet. I did not think she could grow much bigger and still manage to walk. She moved down the hallway like a ship with its sails full, holding on to her bunch of keys so that they wouldn't clink, and disappeared into the great hall.

Later I asked Tanneke why Catharina had been hiding.

"Oh, van Leeuwenhoek was here," she

answered, chuckling. "A friend of the master's. She's afraid of him."

"Why?"

Tanneke laughed harder. "She broke his box! She was looking in it and knocked it over. You know how clumsy she is."

I thought of my mother's knife spinning across the floor. "What box?"

"He has a wooden box that you look in and—see things."

"What things?"

"All sorts of things!" Tanneke replied impatiently. She clearly did not want to talk about the box. "Young mistress broke it, and van Leeuwenhoek won't see her now. That's why master won't allow her in his room unless he's there. Perhaps he thinks she'll knock over a painting!"

I discovered what the box was the next morning, the day he spoke to me about things that took me many months to understand.

When I arrived to clean the studio, the easel and chair had been moved to one side. The desk was in their place, cleared of papers and prints. On it sat a wooden box about the size of a chest for storing clothes in. A smaller box was attached to one side, with a round object protruding from it.

I did not understand what it was, but I did not dare touch it. I went about my cleaning, glancing over at it now and then as if its use would suddenly become clear to me. I cleaned the corner, then the rest of the room, dusting the box so that I hardly touched it with my cloth.

I cleaned the storeroom and mopped the floor. When I was done I stood in front of the box, arms crossed, moving around to study it.

My back was to the door but I knew suddenly that he was standing there. I wasn't sure whether to turn around or wait for him to speak.

He must have made the door creak, for then I was able to turn and face him. He was leaning against the threshold, wearing a long black robe over his daily clothes. He was watching me curiously, but he did not seem anxious that I might damage his box.

"Do you want to look in it?" he asked. It was the first time he had spoken directly to me since he asked about the vegetables many weeks before.

"Yes, sir. I do," I replied without knowing what I was agreeing to. "What is it?"

"It is called a camera obscura."

The words meant nothing to me. I stood aside and watched him unhook a catch and lift up part of the box's top, which had been divided in two and hinged together. He propped up the lid at an angle so that the box was partly open. There was a bit of glass underneath. He leaned over and peered into the space between the lid and box, then touched the round piece at the end of the smaller box. He seemed to be looking at something, though I didn't think there could be much in the box to take such interest in.

He stood up and gazed at the corner I had cleaned so carefully, then reached over and closed the middle window's shutters, so that

68

the room was lit only by the window in the corner.

Then he took off his robe.

I shifted uneasily from one foot to the other.

He removed his hat, placing it on the chair by the easel, and pulled the robe over his head as he leaned over the box again.

I took a step back and glanced at the doorway behind me. Catharina had little will to climb the stairs these days, but I wondered what Maria Thins, or Cornelia, or anyone would think if they saw us. When I turned back I kept my eyes fixed on his shoes, which were gleaming from the polish I had given them the day before.

He stood up at last and pulled the robe from his head, his hair ruffled. "There, Griet, it is ready. Now you look." He stepped away from the box and gestured me towards it. I stood rooted to my place.

"Sir—"

"Place the robe over your head as I did. Then the image will be stronger. And look at it from this angle so it will not be upside down."

I did not know what to do. The thought of me covered with his robe, unable to see, and him looking at me all the while, made me feel faint.

But he was my master. I was meant to do as he said.

I pressed my lips together, then stepped up to the box, to the end where the lid had been lifted. I bent over and looked in at the square of milky glass fixed inside. There was a faint drawing of something on it.

He draped his robe gently over my head so that it blocked out all light. It was still warm from him, and smelled of the way brick feels when it has been baked by the sun. I placed my hands on the table to steady myself and closed my eyes for a moment. I felt as if I had drunk my evening beer too quickly.

"What do you see?" I heard him say.

I opened my eyes and saw the painting, without the woman in it.

"Oh!" I stood up so suddenly that the robe dropped from my head to the floor. I stepped back from the box, treading on the cloth.

I moved my foot. "I'm sorry, sir. I will wash the robe this morning."

"Never mind about the robe, Griet. What did you see?"

I swallowed. I was terribly confused, and a little frightened. What was in the box was a trick of the devil, or something Catholic I did not understand. "I saw the painting, sir. Except that the woman wasn't in it, and it was smaller. And things were—switched around."

"Yes, the image is projected upside down, and left and right are reversed. There are mirrors that can fix that."

I did not understand what he was saying.

"But—"

"What is it?"

"I don't understand, sir. How did it get there?"

He picked up the robe and brushed it off. He was smiling. When he smiled his face was like an open window.

"Do you see this?" He pointed to the round object at the end of the smaller box. "This is called a lens. It is made of a piece of glass cut in a certain way. When light from that scene"—he pointed to the corner—"goes through it and into the box it projects the image so that we can see it here." He tapped the cloudy glass.

I was staring at him so hard, trying to understand, that my eyes began to water.

"What is an image, sir? It is not a word I know."

Something changed in his face, as if he had been looking over my shoulder but now was looking at me. "It is a picture, like a painting."

I nodded. More than anything I wanted him to think I could follow what he said.

"Your eyes are very wide," he said then.

I blushed. "So I have been told, sir."

"Do you want to look again?"

I did not, but I knew I could not say so. I thought for a moment. "I will look again, sir, but only if I am left alone."

He looked surprised, then amused. "All right," he said. He handed me his robe. "I'll return in a few minutes, and tap on the door before I enter."

He left, closing the door behind him. I grasped his robe, my hands shaking.

For a moment I thought of simply pretending to look, and saying that I had. But he would know I was lying.

And I was curious. It became easier to consider it without him watching me. I took a deep breath and gazed down into the box. I could see on the glass a faint trace of the scene in the corner. As I brought the robe over my head the image, as he called it, became clearer and clearer—the table, the chairs, the yellow curtain in the corner, the back wall with the map hanging on it, the ceramic pot gleaming on the table, the pewter basin, the powder-brush, the letter. They were all there, assembled before my eyes on a flat surface, a painting that was not a painting. I cautiously touched the glass—it was smooth and cold, with no traces of paint on it. I removed the robe and the image went faint again, though it was still there. I put the robe over me once more, closing out the light, and watched the jeweled colors appear again. They seemed to be even brighter and more colorful on the glass than they were in the corner.

It became as hard to stop looking into the box as it had been to take my eyes from the painting of the woman with the pearl necklace the first time I'd seen it. When I heard the tap on the door I just had time to straighten up and let the robe drop to my shoulders before he walked in.

"Have you looked again, Griet? Have you looked properly?"

"I have looked, sir, but I am not at all sure of what I have seen." I smoothed my cap.

"It is surprising, isn't it? I was as amazed as you the first time my friend showed it to me."

"But why do you look at it, sir, when you can look at your own painting?"

"You do not understand." He tapped the box.

"This is a tool. I use it to help me see, so that I am able to make the painting."

"But—you use your eyes to see."

"True, but my eyes do not always see everything."

My eyes darted to the corner, as if they would discover something unexpected that had been hidden from me before, behind the powder-brush, emerging from the shadows of the blue cloth.

"Tell me, Griet," he continued, "do you think I simply paint what is there in that corner?"

I glanced at the painting, unable to answer. I felt as if I were being tricked. Whatever I answered would be wrong.

"The camera obscura helps me to see in a different way," he explained. "To see more of what is there."

When he saw the baffled expression on my face he must have regretted saying so much to someone like me. He turned and snapped the box shut. I slipped off his robe and held it out to him.

"Sir—"

"Thank you, Griet," he said as he took it from me. "Have you finished with the cleaning here?"

"Yes, sir."

"You may go, then."

"Thank you, sir." I quickly gathered my cleaning things and left, the door clicking shut behind me.

I thought about what he had said, about how the box helped him to see more. Although I did not understand why, I knew he was right because I could see it in his painting of the woman, and also what I remembered of the painting of Delft. He saw things in a way that others did not, so that a city I had lived in all my life seemed a different place, so that a woman became beautiful with the light on her face.

The day after I looked in the box I went to the studio and it was gone. The easel was back in its place. I glanced at the painting. Previously I had found only tiny changes in it. Now there was one easily seen—the map hanging on the wall behind the woman had been removed from both the painting and the scene itself. The wall was now bare. The painting looked the better for it—simpler, the lines of the woman clearer now against the brownish-white background of the wall. But the change upset me—it was so sudden. I would not have expected it of him.

I felt uneasy after I left the studio, and as I walked to the Meat Hall I did not look about me as I usually did. Though I waved hello to the old butcher I did not stop, even when he called out to me.

Pieter the son was minding the stall alone. I had seen him a few times since that first day, but always in the presence of his father, standing in the background while Pieter the father took charge. Now he said, "Hello, Griet. I've wondered when you would come."

I thought that a silly thing to say, as I had been buying meat at the same time each day.

His eyes did not meet mine.

I decided not to remark on his words. "Three pounds of stewing beef, please. And do you have more of those sausages your father sold me the other day? The girls liked them."

"There are none left, I'm afraid."

A woman came to stand behind me, waiting her turn. Pieter the son glanced at her. "Can you wait for a moment?" he said to me in a low voice.

"Wait?"

"I want to ask you something."

I stood aside so that he could serve the woman. I did not like doing so when I was feeling so unsettled, but I had little choice.

When he was done and we were alone again he asked, "Where does your family live?"

"The Oude Langendijck, at Papists' Corner."

"No, no, *your* family."

I flushed at my mistake. "Off the Rietveld Canal, not far from the Koe Gate. Why do you ask?"

His eyes fully met mine at last. "There have been reports of the plague in that quarter."

I took a step back, my eyes widening. "Has a quarantine been set?"

"Not yet. They expect to today."

Afterwards I realized he must have been asking others about me. If he hadn't already known where my family lived, he would never have known to tell me about the plague.

I do not remember getting back from there. Pieter the son must have placed the meat in my pail but all I knew was that I arrived at the house, dropped the pail at Tanneke's feet and said, "I must see the mistress."

Tanneke rummaged through the pail. "No sausages, and nothing to take their place! What's the matter with you? Go straight back to the Meat Hall."

"I must see the mistress," I repeated.

"What is it?" Tanneke grew suspicious. "Have you done something wrong?"

"My family may be quarantined. I must go to them."

"Oh." Tanneke shifted uncertainly. "I wouldn't know about that. You'll have to ask. She's in with my mistress."

Catharina and Maria Thins were in the Crucifixion room. Maria Thins was smoking her pipe. They stopped talking when I entered.

"What is it, girl?" Maria Thins grunted.

"Please, madam," I addressed Catharina, "I have heard that my family's street may be quarantined. I would like to go and see them."

"What, and bring the plague back with you?" she snapped. "Certainly not. Are you mad?"

I looked at Maria Thins, which made Catharina angrier. "I have said no," she announced. "It is *I* who decide what you can and cannot do. Have you forgotten that?"

"No, madam." I lowered my eyes.

"You won't be going home Sundays until it's safe. Now go, we have things to discuss without you hanging about."

I took the washing to the courtyard and sat outside with my back to the door so that I would not have to see anyone. I wept as I scrubbed one of Maertge's dresses. When I smelled Maria Thins' pipe I wiped my eyes but did not turn round.

"Don't be silly, girl," Maria Thins said quietly to my back. "You can't do anything for them and you have to save yourself. You're a clever girl, you can work that out."

I did not answer. After a while I could no longer smell her pipe.

The next morning he came in while I was sweeping the studio.

"Griet, I am sorry to hear of your family's misfortune," he said.

I looked up from my broom. There was kindness in his eyes, and I felt I could ask him. "Will you tell me, sir, if the quarantine has been set?"

"It was, yesterday morning."

"Thank you for telling me, sir."

He nodded, and was about to leave when I said, "May I ask you something else, sir? About the painting."

He stopped in the doorway. "What is it?"

"When you looked in the box, did it tell you to remove the map from the painting?"

"Yes, it did." His face became intent like a stork's when it sees a fish it can catch. "Does it please you that the map is gone?"

"It is a better painting now." I did not think I would have dared to say such a thing at another time, but the danger to my family had made me reckless.

His smile made me grip my broom tightly.

I was not able to work well then. I was worried about my family, not about how clean I could get the floors or how white the sheets. No one may have remarked on my good housekeeping before, but everyone noticed how careless I was now. Lisbeth complained of a spotted apron. Tanneke grumbled that my sweeping caused dust to settle on the dishes. Catharina shouted at me several times—for forgetting to iron the sleeves of her chemise, for buying cod when I was meant to get herring, for letting the fire go out.

Maria Thins muttered, "Steady yourself, girl," as she passed me in the hallway.

Only in the studio was I able to clean as I had before, maintaining the precision he needed.

I did not know what to do that first Sunday I was not allowed to go home. I could not go to our church either, as it was in the quarantined area as well. I did not want to remain at the house, though—whatever Catholics did on Sundays, I did not want to be among them.

They left together to go to the Jesuit church around the corner in the Molenpoort, the girls wearing good dresses, even Tanneke changed into a yellowish brown wool dress, and carrying Johannes. Catharina walked slowly, holding on to her husband's arm. Maria Thins locked the door behind her. I stood on the tiles in front of the house as they disappeared and considered what to do. The bells in the New Church tower in front of me began to sound the hour.

I was baptized there, I thought. Surely they will allow me inside for the service.

I crept into the vast place, feeling like a mouse hiding in a rich man's house. It was cool and dim inside, the smooth round pillars reaching up, the ceiling so high above me it could almost be the sky. Behind the minister's altar was the grand marble tomb of William of Orange.

I saw no one I knew, only people dressed in sober clothes much finer in their cloth and cut than any I would ever wear. I hid behind a pillar for the service, which I could hardly listen to, I was so nervous that someone would come along and ask me what I was doing there. At the end of the service I slipped out quickly before anyone approached me. I walked round the church and looked across the canal at the house. The door was still shut and locked. Catholic services must last longer than ours, I thought.

I walked as far as I could towards my family's house, stopping only where a barrier manned by a soldier blocked the way. The streets looked very quiet beyond it.

"How is it," I asked the soldier, "back there?"

He shrugged and did not reply. He looked hot in his cloak and hat, for though the sun was not out the air was warm and close.

"Is there a list? Of those who have died?" I could barely say the words.

"Not yet."

I was not surprised—the lists were always delayed, and usually incomplete. Word of mouth was often more accurate. "Do you know—have you heard if Jan the tiler—"

"I know nothing of anyone in there. You'll have to wait." The soldier turned away as others approached him with similar queries.

I tried to speak to another soldier on a barrier at a different street. Though friendlier, he too could tell me nothing about my family. "I could ask around, but not for nothing," he added, smiling and looking me up and down so I would know he didn't mean money.

"Shame on you," I snapped, "for seeking to take advantage of those in misery."

But he did not seem ashamed. I had forgotten that soldiers think of just one thing when they see a young woman.

When I got back to the Oude Langendijck I was relieved to find the house open. I slipped inside and spent the afternoon hiding in the courtyard with my prayer book. In the evening I crept into bed without eating, telling Tanneke my stomach hurt.

At the butcher's Pieter the son pulled me to one side while his father was busy with someone else. "Have you had news of your family?"

I shook my head. "No one could tell me anything." I did not meet his gaze. His concern made me feel as if I had just stepped off a boat and the ground was wobbling under my feet.

"I will find out for you," Pieter stated. From his tone it was clear that I was not to argue with him.

"Thank you," I said after a long pause. I wondered what I would do if he did find out something. He was not demanding anything the way the soldier had, but I would be obliged to him. I did not want to be obliged to anyone.

"It may take a few days," Pieter murmured before he turned to hand his father a cow's liver. He wiped his hands on his apron. I nodded, my eyes on his hands. The creases between his nails and his fingers were filled with blood.

I expect I will have to get used to that sight, I thought.

I began to look forward to my daily errand even more than to cleaning the studio. I dreaded it too, though, especially the moment Pieter the son looked up from his work and saw me, and I searched his eyes for clues. I wanted to know, yet as long as I didn't, it was possible to hope.

Several days passed when I bought meat from him, or passed by his stall after I had bought fish, and he simply shook his head. Then one day he looked up and looked away, and I knew what he would say. I just did not know who.

I had to wait until he finished with several customers. I felt so sick I wanted to sit down, but the floor was speckled with blood.

At last Pieter the son took off his apron and came over. "It is your sister, Agnes," he said softly. "She is very ill."

"And my parents?"

"They stay well, so far."

I did not ask what risk he had gone to in order to find out for me. "Thank you, Pieter," I whispered. It was the first time I had spoken his name.

I looked into his eyes and saw kindness there. I also saw what I had feared—expectation.

On Sunday I decided to visit my brother. I did not know how much he knew of the quarantine or of Agnes. I left the house early and walked to his factory, which was outside the city walls not far from the Rotterdam Gate. Frans was still asleep when I arrived. The woman who answered at the gate laughed when I asked for him. "He'll be asleep for hours yet," she said. "They sleep all day on Sundays, the apprentices. It's their day off."

I did not like her tone, nor what she said. "Please wake him and tell him his sister is here," I demanded. I sounded a bit like Catharina.

The woman raised her eyebrows. "I didn't know Frans came from a family so high on their throne you can see up their noses." She disappeared and I wondered if she would bother to wake Frans. I sat on a low wall to wait. A family passed me on their way to church. The children, two girls and two boys, ran ahead of their parents, just as we had ours. I watched them until they passed from sight.

Frans appeared at last, rubbing sleep from his face. "Oh, Griet," he said. "I didn't know if it would be you or Agnes. I suppose Agnes wouldn't come so far on her own."

He didn't know. I couldn't keep it from him, not even to tell him gently.

"Agnes has been struck by the plague," I blurted out. "God help her and our parents."

Frans stopped rubbing his face. His eyes were red.

"Agnes?" he repeated in confusion. "How do you know this?"

"Someone found out for me."

"You haven't seen them?"

"There is a quarantine."

"A quarantine? How long has there been one?"

"Ten days so far."

Frans shook his head angrily. "I heard nothing of this! Stuck in this factory day after day, nothing but white tiles as far as I can see. I think I may go mad."

"It's Agnes you should be thinking of now."

Frans hung his head unhappily. He had grown taller since I'd seen him months before. His voice had deepened as well.

"Frans, have you been going to church?"

He shrugged. I could not bring myself to question him further.

"I'm going now to pray for them all," I said instead. "Will you come with me?"

He did not want to, but I managed to persuade him—I did not want to face a strange church alone again. We found one not far away, and although the service did not comfort me, I prayed hard for our family.

Afterwards Frans and I walked along the Schie River. We said little, but we each knew what the other was thinking—neither of us had heard of anyone recovering from the plague.

One morning when Maria Thins was unlocking the studio for me she said, "All right, girl. Clear that corner today." She pointed to the area that he was painting. I did not understand what she meant. "All the things on the table should go into the chests in the storeroom," she continued, "except the bowl and Catharina's powder-brush. I'll take them with me." She crossed to the table and picked up two of the objects I had spent so many weeks setting carefully in their places.

When she saw my face Maria Thins laughed. "Don't worry. He's finished. He doesn't need this now. When you're done here make sure you dust all the chairs and set them out by the middle window. And open all the shutters." She left, cradling the pewter bowl in her arms.

Without the bowl and brush the tabletop was transformed into a picture I did not recognize. The letter, the cloth, the ceramic pot lay without meaning, as if someone had simply dropped them onto the table. Still, I could not imagine moving them.

I put off doing so by going about my other duties. I opened all the shutters, which made the room very bright and strange, then dusted and mopped everywhere but the table. I looked at the painting for some time, trying to discover what was different about it that now made it complete. I had seen no changes in it over the past several days.

I was still pondering when he entered. "Griet, you've not yet cleared up. Be quick about it—I've come to help you move the table."

"I'm sorry for being so slow, sir. It's just—" He seemed surprised that I wanted to say something—"I'm so used to the objects where they are that I hate to move them."

"I see. I will help you, then." He plucked the blue cloth from the table and held it out. His hands were very clean. I took the cloth from him without touching them and brought it to the window to shake out. Then I folded it and placed it in a chest in the storeroom. When I came back he had gathered up the letter and the black ceramic pot and stored them away. We moved the table to the side of the room and I set up the chairs by the middle while he moved the easel and painting to the corner where the scene had been set.

It was odd to see the painting in the place of the setting. It all felt strange, this sudden movement and change after weeks of stillness and quiet. It was not like him. I did not ask him why. I wanted to look at him, to guess what he was thinking, but I kept my eyes on my broom, cleaning up the dust disturbed by the blue cloth.

He left me and I finished up quickly, not wanting to linger in the studio. It was no longer comforting there.

That afternoon van Ruijven and his wife visited. Tanneke and I were sitting on the bench in front while she showed me how to mend some lace cuffs. The girls had gone over to Market Square and were flying a kite near the New Church where we could see them, Maertge holding the end of the string while Cornelia tugged the kite up into the sky.

I saw the van Ruijvens coming from a long way off. As they approached I recognized her from the painting and my brief meeting with her, and him as the moustached man with the white feather in his hat and the oily smile who had once escorted her to the door.

"Look, Tanneke," I whispered, "it's the gentleman who admires the painting of you every day."

"Oh!" Tanneke blushed when she saw them. Straightening her cap and apron, she hissed, "Go and tell mistress they're here!"

I ran inside and found Maria Thins and Catharina with the sleeping baby in the Cru-

cifixion room. "The van Ruijvens have come,"
I announced.

Catharina and Maria Thins removed their
caps and smoothed their collars. Catharina held
on to the table and pulled herself up. As they
were leaving the room Maria Thins reached
up and straightened one of Catharina's tortoiseshell combs, which she only wore on
special occasions.

They greeted their guests in the front hall
while I hovered in the hallway. As they moved
to the stairs van Ruijven caught sight of me
and paused for a moment.

"Who's this, then?"

Catharina frowned at me. "Just one of the
maids. Tanneke, bring us up some wine,
please."

"Have the wide-eyed maid bring it to us,"
van Ruijven commanded. "Come, my dear,"
he said to his wife, who began climbing the
stairs.

Tanneke and I stood side by side, she
annoyed, me dismayed by his attention.

"Go on, then!" Catharina cried to me.
"You heard what he said. Bring the wine." She
pulled herself heavily up the stairs after Maria
Thins.

I went to the little room where the girls
slept, found glasses stored there, polished
five of them with my apron and set them on
a tray. Then I searched the kitchen for wine.
I did not know where it was kept, for they did
not drink wine often. Tanneke had disappeared in a huff. I feared the wine was kept

locked away in one of the cupboards, and that I would have to ask Catharina for the key in front of everyone.

Fortunately, Maria Thins must have anticipated this. In the Crucifixion room she left out a white jug with a pewter top, filled with wine. I set it on the tray and carried it up to the studio, first straightening my cap, collar and apron as the others had done.

When I entered they were standing by the painting. "A jewel once again," van Ruijven was saying. "Are you happy with it, my dear?" he addressed his wife.

"Of course," she answered. The light was shining through the windows onto her face and she looked almost beautiful.

As I set the tray down on the table my master and I had moved that morning Maria Thins came over. "I'll take that," she whispered. "Off you go. Quickly, now."

I was on the stairs when I heard van Ruijven say, "Where's that wide-eyed maid? Gone already? I wanted to have a proper look at her."

"Now, now, she's nothing!" Catharina cried gaily. "It's the painting you want to look at."

I went back to the front bench and took my seat next to Tanneke, who wouldn't say a word to me. We sat in silence, working on the cuffs, listening to the voices floating out from the windows above.

When they came down again I slipped around the corner and waited, leaning against the warm bricks of a wall in the Molenpoort, until they were gone.

Later a man servant from their house came and disappeared up to the studio. I did not see him go, as the girls had come back and wanted me to build up the fire so they could bake apples in it.

The next morning the painting was gone. I had not had a chance to look at it one last time.

That morning as I arrived at the Meat Hall I heard a man ahead of me say the quarantine had been lifted. I hurried to Pieter's stall. Father and son were both there, and several people were waiting to be served. I ignored them and went straight up to Pieter the son. "Can you serve me quickly?" I said. "I must go to my family's house. Just three pounds of tongue and three of sausages."

He stopped what he had been doing, ignoring the indignant sounds from the old woman he had been helping. "I suppose if I were young and smiled at you you'd do anything for me too," she scolded as he handed the packages to me.

"She's not smiling," Pieter replied. He glanced at his father, then handed me a smaller package. "For your family," he said in a low voice.

I did not even thank him—I snatched the package and ran.

Only thieves and children run.

I ran all the way home.

My parents were sitting side by side on the

bench, heads bowed. When I reached them I took my father's hand and raised it to my cheek. I sat next to them and said nothing.

There was nothing to be said.

There followed a time when everything was dull. The things that had meant something—the cleanness of the laundry, the daily walk on errands, the quiet studio—lost importance, though they were still there, like bruises on the body that fade to hard lumps under the skin.

It was at the end of the summer that my sister died. That autumn was rainy. I spent much of my time hanging laundry on racks indoors, shifting them closer to the fire, trying to dry the clothes before mildew took over but without scorching them.

Tanneke and Maria Thins treated me kindly enough when they found out about Agnes. Tanneke managed to check her irritation for several days, though soon she began again to scold and sulk, leaving it to me to placate her. Maria Thins said little but took to cutting off her daughter when Catharina became sharp with me.

Catharina herself seemed to know nothing of my sister, or did not show it. She was nearing her confinement, and as Tanneke had predicted she spent most of her time in bed, leaving the baby Johannes to Maertge's charge. He was beginning to toddle about, and kept the girls busy.

The girls did not know I had a sister and so would not understand that I could lose one. Only Aleydis seemed to sense that something was wrong. She sometimes came to sit by me, pushing her body close to mine like a pup burrowing into its mother's fur for warmth. She comforted me in a simple way that no one else could.

One day Cornelia came out to the courtyard where I was hanging up clothes. She held out an old doll to me. "We don't play with this anymore," she announced. "Not even Aleydis. Would you like to give it to your sister?" She made her eyes wide and innocent, and I knew she must have overheard someone mention Agnes' death.

"No, thank you," was all I could say, almost choking on the words.

She smiled and skipped away.

The studio remained empty. He did not start another painting. He spent much of his time away from the house, either at the Guild or at Mechelen, his mother's inn across the square. I still cleaned the studio, but it became like any other task, just another room to mop and dust.

When I visited the Meat Hall I found it hard to meet Pieter the son's eye. His kindness pained me. I should have returned it but did not. I should have been flattered but was not. I did not want his attention. I came to prefer being served by his father, who teased me but did not demand anything from me but to be critical of his meat. We ate fine meat that autumn.

On Sundays I sometimes went to Frans' factory and urged him to come home with me. He did twice, cheering my parents a little. Until a year before they'd had three children at home. Now they had none. When Frans and I were both there we reminded them of better times. Once my mother even laughed, before stopping herself with a shake of her head. "God has punished us for taking for granted our good fortune," she said. "We must not forget that."

It was not easy visiting home. I found that after staying away those few Sundays during the quarantine, home had come to feel like a strange place. I was beginning to forget where my mother kept things, what kind of tiles lined the fireplace, how the sun shone in the rooms at different times of the day. After only a few months I could describe the house in Papists' Corner better than my family's.

Frans especially found it hard to visit. After long days and nights at the factory he wanted to smile and laugh and tease, or at least to sleep. I suppose I coaxed him there hoping to knit our family together again. It was impossible, though. Since my father's accident we had become a different family.

When I came back one Sunday from my parents', Catharina had begun her labor. I heard her groaning when I stepped inside the front door. I peeked into the great hall, which was darker than usual—the lower windows had been shuttered to give her privacy. Maria Thins was there with Tanneke and the midwife. When Maria Thins saw me she said, "Go look for the girls—I've sent them out to play. It won't be long now. Come back in an hour."

I was glad to leave. Catharina was making a great deal of noise, and it did not seem right to listen to her in that state. I knew too that she would not want me there.

I looked for the girls in their favorite place, the Beast Market round the corner from us, where livestock was sold. When I found them they were playing marbles and chasing one another. Baby Johannes tumbled after them—unsteady on his feet, he half walked, half crawled. It was not the kind of play we would have been allowed on a Sunday, but Catholics held different views.

When Aleydis grew tired she came to sit with me. "Will Mama have the baby soon?" she asked.

"Your grandmother said she would. We'll go back in a bit and see them."

"Will Papa be pleased?"

"I should think so."

"Will he paint more quickly now there's another baby?"

I did not answer. Catharina's words were coming from a little girl's mouth. I did not want to hear more.

When we returned he was standing in the doorway. "Papa, your cap!" cried Cornelia. The girls ran up to him and tried to snatch off the quilted paternity cap he wore, its ribbons dangling below his ears. He looked both proud and embarrassed. I was surprised—he had become a father five times before, and I thought he would be used to it. There was no reason for him to be embarrassed.

It is Catharina who wants many children, I thought then. He would rather be alone in his studio.

But that could not be quite right. I knew how babies were made. He had his part to play, and he must have played it willingly. And as difficult as Catharina could be, I had often seen him look at her, touch her shoulder, speak to her in a low voice laced with honey.

I did not like to think of him in that way, with his wife and children. I preferred to think of him alone in his studio. Or not alone, but with only me.

"You have another brother, girls," he said. "His name is Franciscus. Would you like to see him?" He led them inside while I hung back in the street, holding Johannes.

Tanneke opened the shutters of the great hall's lower windows and leaned out.

"Is the mistress all right?" I asked.

"Oh, yes. She makes a racket but there's nothing behind it. She's made to have babies—pops them out like a chestnut from its shell. Now come, master wants to say a prayer of thanks."

Though uncomfortable, I could not refuse to pray with them. Protestants would have done the same after a good birth. I carried Johannes into the great hall, which was much lighter now and full of people. When I set him down he tottered over to his sisters, who were gathered around the bed. The curtains had been drawn back and Catharina lay propped against pillows, cradling the baby. Though exhausted, she was smiling, happy for once. My master stood near her, gazing down at his new son. Aleydis was holding his hand. Tanneke and the midwife were clearing away basins and bloody sheets while the new nurse waited near the bed.

Maria Thins came in from one of the kitchens with some wine and three glasses on a tray. When she set them down he let go of Aleydis' hand, stepped away from the bed, and he and Maria Thins kneeled. Tanneke and the midwife stopped what they were doing and kneeled as well. Then the nurse and children and I kneeled, Johannes squirming and crying out as Lisbeth forced him to sit.

My master said a prayer to God, thanking Him for the safe delivery of Franciscus and for sparing Catharina. He added some Catholic phrases in Latin which I did not understand, but I did not mind much—he had a low, soothing voice that I liked to listen to.

When he was done Maria Thins poured three glasses of wine and she and he and Catharina drank good health to the baby. Then Catharina handed the baby to the nurse, who put him to her breast.

Tanneke signalled to me and we left the room to get bread and smoked herring for the midwife and the girls. "We'll begin preparing for the birth feast now," Tanneke remarked as we were setting things out. "Young mistress likes a big one. We'll be run off our feet as usual."

The birth feast was the biggest celebration I was to witness in that house. We had ten days to prepare for it, ten days of cleaning and cooking. Maria Thins hired two girls for a week to help Tanneke with the food and me with the cleaning. My girl was slow witted but worked well as long as I told her exactly what to do and kept a close eye on her. One day we washed—whether they were clean already or not—all the tablecloths and napkins that would be needed for the feast, as well as all the clothes in the house—shirts, robes, bonnets, collars, handkerchiefs, caps, aprons. The linens took another day. Then we washed all the tankards, glasses, earthenware plates, jugs, copper pots, pancake pans, iron grills and spits, spoons, ladles, as well as those from the neighbors, who lent them for the occasion. We polished the brass and the copper and the silver. We took curtains down and shook them outside, and beat all the cushions and rugs. We polished the wood of the beds, the cupboards, the chairs and tables, the windowsills, until everything gleamed.

By the end my hands were cracked and bleeding.

It was very clean for the feast.

Maria Thins placed special orders for lamb and veal and tongue, for a whole pig, for hare and pheasant and capons, for oysters and lobsters and caviar and herring, for sweet wine and the best ale, for sweet cakes prepared specially by the baker.

When I placed the meat order for Maria Thins with Pieter the father, he rubbed his hands. "So, yet another mouth to feed," he proclaimed. "All the better for us!"

Great wheels of Gouda and Edam arrived, and artichokes and oranges and lemons and grapes and plums, and almonds and hazelnuts. Even a pineapple was sent, gift of a wealthy cousin of Maria Thins. I had never seen one before, and was not tempted by its rough, prickly skin. It was not for me to eat anyway. None of the food was, except for the odd taste Tanneke allowed us. She let me try a tiny bit of caviar, which I liked less than I admitted, for all its luxury, and some of the sweet wine, which was wonderfully spiced with cinnamon.

Extra peat and wood were piled in the courtyard, and spits borrowed from a neighbor. Barrels of ale were also kept in the courtyard, and the pig was roasted there. Maria Thins hired a young boy to look after all the fires, which were in use all night once we began roasting the pig.

Throughout the preparations Catharina remained in bed with Franciscus, tended by the nurse, serene as a swan. Like a swan too, though, she had a long neck and sharp beak. I kept away from her.

"This is how she would like the house to be every day," Tanneke grumbled to me as she was preparing jugged hare and I was boiling water to wash the windows with. "She wants everything to be in a state around her. Queen of the bedcovers!" I chuckled with her, knowing I shouldn't encourage her to be disloyal but cheered none the less when she was.

He stayed away during the preparations, locked in his studio or escaping to the Guild. I saw him only once, three days before the feast. The hired girl and I were polishing candlesticks in the kitchen when Lisbeth came to find me. "Butcher's asking for you," she said. "Out front."

I dropped the polishing cloth, wiped my hands on my apron and followed her up the hallway. I knew it would be the son. He had never seen me in Papists' Corner. At least my face was not chapped and red as it normally was from hanging over the steaming laundry.

Pieter the son had pulled up a cart in front of the house, loaded with the meat Maria Thins had ordered. The girls were peering into it. Only Cornelia looked round. When I appeared in the doorway Pieter smiled at me. I remained calm and did not blush. Cornelia was watching me.

She was not the only one. I felt his presence at my back—he had come down the hallway behind me. I turned to look at him, and saw that he had seen Pieter's smile, and the expectation there as well.

He transferred his grey eyes to me. They were cold. I felt dizzy, as if I had stood up too quickly. I turned back round. Pieter's smile was not so wide now. He had seen my dizziness.

I felt caught between the two men. It was not a pleasant feeling.

I stood aside to let my master pass. He turned into the Molenpoort without a word or glance. Pieter and I watched him go in silence.

"I have your order," Pieter said then. "Where would you like it?"

That Sunday when I went home to my parents I did not want to tell them that another child had been born. I thought it would remind them of losing Agnes. But my mother had heard of it at the market and so I was made to describe to them the birth and praying with the family and all the preparations that had been made so far for the feast. My mother was concerned about the state of my hands, but I promised her the worst was done.

"And a painting?" my father asked. "Has he begun another painting?" He always hoped that I would describe a new painting to him.

"Nothing," I replied. I had spent little time in the studio that week. Nothing there had changed.

"Perhaps he is idle," my mother said.

"He is not that," I answered quickly.

"Perhaps he does not want to see," my father said.

"I don't know what he wants," I said more sharply than I had intended. My mother gazed at me. My father shifted in his seat.

I said nothing more about him.

The guests began to arrive around noon on the feast day. By evening there were perhaps a hundred people in and out of the house, spilling into the courtyard and the street. All sorts had been invited—wealthy merchants as well as our baker, tailor, cobbler, apothecary. Neighbors were there, and my master's mother and sister, and Maria Thins' cousins. Painters were there, and other Guild members. Van Leeuwenhoek was there, and van Ruijven and his wife.

Even Pieter the father was there, without his blood-stained apron, nodding and smiling at me as I passed with a jug of spiced wine. "Well, Griet," he said as I poured him some, "my son will be jealous that I'm spending the evening with you."

"I think not," I murmured, pulling away from him, embarrassed.

Catharina was the center of attention. She had on a green silk dress altered to accommodate her belly, which had not yet shrunk. Over it she wore the ermine-trimmed yellow mantle van Ruijven's wife had worn for the painting. It was odd to see it around another woman's shoulders. I didn't like her wearing it, though it was of course hers to wear. She also wore a pearl necklace and earrings, and her blond curls were dressed prettily. She had recovered quickly from the birth, and was very merry and graceful, her body relieved of some of the burden it had been carrying over the months. She moved easily through the rooms, drinking and laughing with her guests, lighting candles, calling for food, bringing people together. She stopped only to make a fuss over Franciscus when he was being fed by the nurse.

My master was much quieter. He spent most of his time in one corner of the great hall, talking to van Leeuwenhoek, though his eyes often followed Catharina around the room as she moved among her guests. He wore a smart black velvet jacket and his paternity cap, and looked comfortable though not much interested in the party. Large crowds did not appeal to him as they did his wife.

Late in the evening, van Ruijven managed to corner me in the hallway as I was passing along it with a lighted candle and a wine jug. "Ah, the wide-eyed maid," he cried, leaning into me. "Hello, my girl." He grabbed my chin in his hand, his other hand pulling the candle up to light my face. I did not like the way he looked at me.

"You should paint her," he said over his shoulder.

My master was there. He was frowning. He looked as if he wanted to say something to his patron but could not.

"Griet, get me some more wine." Pieter the father had popped out from the Crucifixion room and was holding a cup towards me.

"Yes, sir." I pulled my chin from van Ruijven's grasp and quickly crossed to Pieter the father. I could feel two pairs of eyes on my back.

"Oh, I'm sorry, sir, the jug's empty. I'll just get some more from the kitchen." I hurried away, holding the jug close so they would not discover that it was full.

When I returned a few minutes later only Pieter the father remained, leaning against the wall. "Thank you," I said in a low voice as I filled his glass.

He winked at me. "It was worth it just to hear you call me sir. I'll never hear that again, will I?" He raised his glass in a mock toast and drank.

After the feast winter descended on us, and the house became cold and flat. Besides a great deal of cleaning up, there was no longer something to look forward to. The girls, even Aleydis, became difficult, demanding attention, rarely helping. Maria Thins spent longer in her own rooms upstairs than she had before. Franciscus, who had remained quiet all the way through the feast, suffered from wind and began to cry almost constantly. He made a piercing sound that could be heard throughout the house—in the courtyard, in the studio, in the cellar. Given her nature, Catharina was surprisingly patient with the baby, but snapped at everyone else, even her husband.

I had managed to put Agnes from my mind while preparing for the feast, but memories of her returned even more strongly than before. Now that I had time to think, I thought too much. I was like a dog licking its wounds to clean them but making them worse.

Worst of all, he was angry with me. Since the night van Ruijven cornered me, perhaps even since Pieter the son smiled at me, he had become more distant. I seemed also to cross paths with him more often than before. Although he went out a great deal—in part to escape Franciscus' crying—I always seemed to be coming in the front door as he was leaving, or coming down the stairs as he was going up, or sweeping the Crucifixion room when he was looking for Maria Thins there. One day on an errand for Catharina I even met him in Market Square. Each time he nodded politely, then stepped aside to let me pass without looking at me.

I had offended him, but I did not know how.

The studio had become cold and flat as well. Before it had felt busy and full of purpose—it was where paintings were being made. Now, though I quickly swept away any dust that settled, it was simply an empty room, waiting for nothing but dust. I did not want it to be a sad place. I wanted to take refuge there, as I had before.

One morning Maria Thins came to open the door for me and found it already unlocked. We peered into the semidarkness. He was asleep at the table, his head on his arms, his back to the door. Maria Thins backed out. "Must have come up here because of the baby's cries," she muttered. I tried to look again but she was blocking the way. She shut the door softly. "Leave him be. You can clean there later."

The next morning in the studio I opened all the shutters and looked around the room for something I could do, something I could touch that would not offend him, something I could move that he would not notice. Everything was in its place—the table, the chairs, the desk covered with books and papers, the cupboard with the brushes and knife carefully arranged on top, the easel propped against the wall, the clean palettes next to it. The objects he had painted were packed away in the storeroom or back in use in the house.

One of the bells of the New Church began to toll the hour. I went to the window to look out. By the time the bell had finished its sixth stroke I knew what I would do.

I got some water heated on the fire, some soap and clean rags and brought them back to the studio, where I began cleaning the windows. I had to stand on the table to reach the top panes.

I was washing the last window when I heard him enter the room. I turned to look at him over my left shoulder, my eyes wide. "Sir," I began nervously. I was not sure how to explain my impulse to clean.

"Stop."

I froze, horrified that I had gone against his wishes.

"Don't move."

He was staring at me as if a ghost had suddenly appeared in his studio.

"I'm sorry, sir," I said, dropping the rag into the bucket of water. "I should have asked you first. But you are not painting anything at the moment and—"

He looked puzzled, then shook his head. "Oh, the windows. No, you may continue what you were doing."

I would rather not have cleaned in front of him, but as he continued to stand there I had no choice. I swished the rag in the water, wrung it out and began wiping the panes again, inside and out.

I finished the window and stepped back to view the effect. The light that shone in was pure.

He was still standing behind me. "Does that please you, sir?" I asked.

"Look over your shoulder at me again."

I did as he commanded. He was studying me. He was interested in me again.

"The light," I said. "It's cleaner now."

"Yes," he said. "Yes."

The next morning the table had been moved back to the painting corner and covered with a red, yellow and blue table rug. A chair was set against the back wall, and a map hung over it.

He had begun again.

1665

My father wanted me to describe the painting once more.

"But nothing has changed since the last time," I said.

"I want to hear it again," he insisted, hunching over in his chair to get nearer to the fire. He sounded like Frans when he was a little boy and had been told there was nothing left to eat in the hotpot. My father was often impatient during March, waiting for winter to end, the cold to ease, the sun to reappear. March was an unpredictable month, when it was never clear what might happen. Warm days raised hopes until ice and grey skies shut over the town again.

March was the month I was born.

Being blind seemed to make my father hate winter even more. His other senses strengthened, he felt the cold acutely, smelled the stale air in the house, tasted the blandness of the vegetable stew more than my mother. He suffered when the winter was long.

I felt sorry for him. When I could I smuggled to him treats from Tanneke's kitchen—stewed cherries, dried apricots, a cold sausage, once a handful of dried rose petals I had found in Catharina's cupboard.

"The baker's daughter stands in a bright corner by a window," I began patiently. "She is facing us, but is looking out the window, down to her right. She is wearing a yellow and black fitted bodice of silk and velvet, a dark blue skirt, and a white cap that hangs down in two points below her chin."

"As you wear yours?" my father asked. He had never asked this before, though I had described the cap the same way each time.

"Yes, like mine. When you look at the cap long enough," I added hurriedly, "you see that he has not really painted it white, but blue, and violet, and yellow."

"But it's a white cap, you said."

"Yes, that's what is so strange. It's painted many colors, but when you look at it, you think it's white."

"Tile painting is much simpler," my father grumbled. "You use blue and that's all. A dark blue for the outlines, a light blue for the shadows. Blue is blue."

And a tile is a tile, I thought, and nothing like his paintings. I wanted him to understand that white was not simply white. It was a lesson my master had taught me.

"What is she doing?" he asked after a moment.

"She has one hand on a pewter pitcher sitting on a table and one on a window she's partly opened. She's about to pick up the pitcher and dump the water from it out the window, but she's stopped in the middle of what she's doing and is either dreaming or looking at something in the street."

"Which is she doing?"

"I don't know. Sometimes it seems one thing, sometimes the other."

My father sat back in his seat, frowning. "First you say the cap is white but not painted white. Then you say the girl is doing one thing or maybe another. You're confusing me." He rubbed his brow as if his head ached.

"I'm sorry, Father. I'm trying to describe it accurately."

"But what is the story in the painting?"

"His paintings don't tell stories."

He did not respond. He had been difficult all winter. If Agnes had been there she would have been able to cheer him. She had always known how to make him laugh.

"Mother, shall I light the footwarmers?" I asked, turning from my father to hide my irritation. Now that he was blind, he could easily sense the moods of others, when he wanted to. I did not like him being critical of the painting without having seen it, or comparing it to the tiles he had once painted. I wanted to tell him that if he could only see the painting he would understand that there was nothing confusing about it. It may not have told a story, but it was still a painting you could not stop looking at.

At the time my father and I talked, my mother had been busy around us, stirring the stew, feeding the fire, setting out plates and mugs, sharpening a knife to cut the bread. Without waiting for her to answer I gathered the footwarmers and took them to the back room where the peat was stored. As I filled them I chided myself for being angry with my father.

I brought the footwarmers back and lit them from the fire. When I had placed them under our seats at the table I led my father over to his chair while my mother spooned out the stew and poured the beer. My father took a bite and made a face. "Didn't you bring anything from Papists' Corner to sweeten this mush?" he muttered.

"I couldn't. Tanneke has been difficult with me and I've stayed away from her kitchen." I regretted it the moment the words left my mouth.

"Why? What did you do?" More and more my father was looking to find fault with me, at times even siding with Tanneke.

I thought quickly. "I spilled some of their best ale. A whole jug."

My mother looked at me reproachfully. She knew when I lied. If my father hadn't been feeling so miserable he might have noticed from my voice as well.

I was getting better at it, though.

When I left to go back my mother insisted on accompanying me part of the way, even though it was raining, a cold, hard rain. As we reached the Rietveld Canal and turned right towards Market Square, she said, "You will be seventeen soon."

"Next week," I agreed.

"Not long now until you are a woman."

"Not long." I kept my eyes on the raindrops pebbling the canal. I did not like to think about the future.

"I have heard that the butcher's son is paying you attention."

"Who told you that?"

In answer she simply brushed raindrops from her cap and shook out her shawl.

I shrugged. "I'm sure he's paying me no more attention than he is other girls."

I expected her to warn me, to tell me to be a good girl, to protect our family name. Instead she said, "Don't be rude to him. Smile at him and be pleasant."

Her words surprised me, but when I looked in her eyes and saw there the hunger for meat that a butcher's son could provide, I understood why she had set aside her pride.

At least she did not ask me about the lie I had told earlier. I could not tell them why Tanneke was angry at me. That lie hid a much greater lie. I would have too much to explain.

Tanneke had discovered what I was doing during the afternoons when I was meant to be sewing.

I was assisting him.

It had begun two months before, one afternoon in January not long after Franciscus was born. It was very cold. Franciscus and Johannes were both poorly, with chesty coughs and trouble breathing. Catharina and the nurse were tending them by the fire in the washing kitchen while the rest of us sat close to the fire in the cooking kitchen.

Only he was not there. He was upstairs. The cold did not seem to affect him.

Catharina came to stand in the doorway between the two kitchens. "Someone must go to the apothecary," she announced, her face flushed. "I need some things for the boys." She looked pointedly at me.

Usually I would be the last chosen for such an errand. Visiting the apothecary was not like going to the butcher's or fishmonger's—tasks Catharina continued to leave to me after the birth of Franciscus. The apothecary was a respected doctor, and Catharina or Maria Thins liked to go to him. I was not allowed such a luxury. When it was so cold, however, any errand was given to the least important member of the house.

For once Maertge and Lisbeth did not ask to come with me. I wrapped myself in a woollen mantle and shawls while Catharina told me I was to ask for dried elder flowers and a coltsfoot elixir. Cornelia hung about, watching me tuck in the loose ends of the shawls.

"May I come with you?" she asked, smiling at me with well-practiced innocence. Sometimes I wondered if I judged her too harshly.

"No," Catharina replied for me. "It's far too cold. I won't have another of my children getting sick. Off you go, then," she said to me. "Quick as you can."

I pulled the front door shut and stepped into the street. It was very quiet—people were sensibly huddled in their houses. The canal was frozen, the sky an angry grey. As the wind blew through me and I drew my nose further into the wool folds around my face, I heard my name being called. I looked around, thinking Cornelia had followed me. The front door was shut.

I looked up. He had opened a window and poked his head out.

"Sir?"

"Where are you going, Griet?"

"To the apothecary, sir. Mistress asked me. For the boys."

"Will you get me something as well?"

"Of course, sir." Suddenly the wind did not seem so bitter.

"Wait, I'll write it down." He disappeared and I waited. After a moment he reappeared and tossed down a small leather pouch. "Give the apothecary the paper inside and bring what he gives you back to me."

I nodded and tucked the pouch into a fold of my shawl, pleased with this secret request.

The apothecary's was along the Koornmarkt, towards the Rotterdam Gate. Although it was not far, each breath I took seemed to freeze inside me so that by the time I pushed into the shop I was unable to speak.

I had never been to an apothecary, not even before I became a maid—my mother had made all of our remedies. His shop was a small room, with shelves lining the walls from floor to ceiling. They held all sizes of bottles, basins and earthenware jars, each one neatly labelled. I suspected that even if I could read the words I would not understand what each vessel held. Although the cold killed most smells, here there lingered an odor I did not recognize, like something in the forest, hidden under rotting leaves.

I had seen the apothecary himself only once, when he came to Franciscus' birth feast a few weeks before. A bald, slight man, he reminded me of a baby bird. He was surprised to see me. Few people ventured out in such cold. He sat behind a table, a set of scales at his elbow, and waited for me to speak.

"I've come for my master and mistress," I gasped at last when my throat had warmed enough for me to speak. He looked blank and I added, "The Vermeers."

"Ah. How is the growing family?"

"The babies are ill. My mistress needs dried elder flowers and an elixir of coltsfoot. And my master—" I handed him the pouch. He took it with a puzzled expression, but when he read the slip of paper he nodded. "Run out of bone black and ocher," he murmured. "That's easily repaired. He's never had anyone fetch the makings of colors for him before, though." He squinted over the slip of paper at me. "He always gets them himself. This is a surprise."

I said nothing.

"Have a seat, then. Back here by the fire while I get your things together." He became busy, opening jars and weighing small mounds of dried flower buds, measuring syrup into a bottle, wrapping things carefully in paper and string. He placed some things in the leather pouch. The other packages he left loose.

"Does he need any canvases?" he asked over his shoulder as he replaced a jar on a high shelf.

"I wouldn't know, sir. He asked me to get only what was on that paper."

"This is very surprising, very surprising indeed." He looked me up and down. I drew myself up—his attention made me wish I were taller. "Well, it is cold, after all. He wouldn't go out unless he had to." He handed me the packages and pouch and held the door open for me. Out in the street I looked back to see him still peering at me through a tiny window in the door.

Back at the house I went first to Catharina to give her the loose packages. Then I hurried to the stairs. He had come down and was waiting. I pulled the pouch from my shawl and handed it to him.

"Thank you, Griet," he said.

"What are you doing?" Cornelia was watching us from further along the hallway.

To my surprise he didn't answer her. He simply turned and climbed the stairs again, leaving me alone to face her.

The truth was the easiest answer, though I often felt uneasy telling Cornelia the truth. I was never sure what she would do with it. "I've bought some paint things for your father," I explained.

"Did he ask you to?"

To that question I responded as her father had—I walked away from her toward the kitchens, removing my shawls as I went. I was afraid to answer, for I did not want to cause him harm. I knew already that it was best if no one knew I had run an errand for him.

I wondered if Cornelia would tell her mother what she had seen. Although young she was also shrewd, like her grandmother. She might hoard her information, carefully choosing when to reveal it.

She gave me her own answer a few days later.

It was a Sunday and I was in the cellar, looking in the chest where I kept my things for a collar to wear that my mother had embroidered for me. I saw immediately that my few belongings had been disturbed—collars not refolded, one of my chemises balled up and pushed into a corner, the tortoiseshell comb shaken from its handkerchief. The handkerchief around my father's tile was folded so neatly that I became suspicious. When I opened it the tile came apart in two pieces. It had been broken so that the girl and boy were separated from each other, the boy now looking behind him at nothing, the girl all alone, her face hidden by her cap.

I wept then. Cornelia could not have guessed how that would hurt me. I would have been less upset if she had broken our heads from our bodies.

He began to ask me to do other things. One day he asked me to buy linseed oil at the apothecary's on my way back from the fish stalls. I was to leave it at the bottom of the stairs for him so that he and the model would not be disturbed. So he said. Perhaps he was aware that Maria Thins or Catharina or Tanneke—or Cornelia—might notice if I went up to the studio at an unusual time.

It was not a house where secrets could be kept easily.

Another day he had me ask the butcher for a pig's bladder. I did not understand why he wanted one until he later asked me to lay out paints he needed each morning when I had finished cleaning. He opened the drawers to the cupboard near his easel and showed me which paints were kept where, naming the colors as he went. I had not heard of many of the words—ultramarine, vermilion, massicot. The brown and yellow earth colors and the bone black and lead white were stored in little earthenware pots, covered with parchment to keep them from drying out. The more valuable colors—the blues and reds and yellows—were kept in small amounts in pigs' bladders. A hole was punched in them so the paint could be squeezed out, with a nail plugging it shut.

One morning while I was cleaning he came in and asked me to stand in for the baker's daughter, who had taken ill and could not come. "I want to look for a moment," he explained. "Someone must stand there."

I obediently took her place, one hand on the handle of the water pitcher, the other on the window frame, opened slightly so that a chilly draft brushed my face and chest.

Perhaps this is why the baker's daughter is ill, I thought.

He had opened all of the shutters. I had never seen the room so bright.

"Tilt your chin down," he said. "And look down, not at me. Yes, that's it. Don't move."

He was sitting by the easel. He did not pick up his palette or his knife or his brushes. He simply sat, hands in his lap, and looked.

My face turned red. I had not realized that he would stare at me so intently.

I tried to think of something else. I looked out the window and watched a boat moving along the canal. The man poling it was the man who had helped me get the pot from the canal my first day. How much has changed since that morning, I thought. I had not even seen one of his paintings then. Now I am standing in one.

"Don't look at what you are looking at," he said. "I can see it in your face. It is distracting you."

I tried not to look at anything, but to think

of other things. I thought of a day when our family went out into the countryside to pick herbs. I thought of a hanging I had seen in Market Square the year before, of a woman who had killed her daughter in a drunken rage. I thought of the look on Agnes' face the last time I had seen her.

"You are thinking too much," he said, shifting in his seat.

I felt as if I had washed a tub full of sheets but not got them clean. "I'm sorry, sir. I don't know what to do."

"Try closing your eyes."

I closed them. After a moment I felt the window frame and the pitcher in my hands, anchoring me. Then I could sense the wall behind me, and the table to my left, and the cold air from the window.

This must be how my father feels, I thought, with the space all around him, and his body knowing where it is.

"Good," he said. "That is good. Thank you, Griet. You may continue cleaning."

I had never seen a painting made from the beginning. I thought that you painted what you saw, using the colors you saw.

He taught me.

He began the painting of the baker's daughter with a layer of pale grey on the white canvas. Then he made reddish-brown marks all over it to indicate where the girl and the table and pitcher and window and map would go. After that I thought he would begin to paint what he saw—a girl's face, a blue skirt, a yellow and black bodice, a brown map, a silver pitcher and basin, a white wall. Instead he painted patches of color—black where her skirt would be, ocher for the bodice and the map on the wall, red for the pitcher and the basin it sat in, another grey for the wall. They were the wrong colors—none was the color of the thing itself. He spent a long time on these false colors, as I called them.

Sometimes the girl came and spent hour after hour standing in place, yet when I looked at the painting the next day nothing had been added or taken away. There were just areas of color that did not make things, no matter how long I studied them. I only knew what they were meant to be because I cleaned the objects themselves, and had seen what the girl was wearing when I peeked at her one day as she changed into Catharina's yellow and black bodice in the great hall.

I reluctantly set out the colors he asked for each morning. One day I put out a blue as well. The second time I laid it out he said to me, "No ultramarine, Griet. Only the colors I asked for. Why did you set it out when I did not ask for it?" He was annoyed.

"I'm sorry, sir. It's just—" I took a deep breath—"she is wearing a blue skirt. I thought you would want it, rather than leaving it black."

"When I am ready, I will ask."

I nodded and turned back to polishing the lion-head chair. My chest hurt. I did not want him to be angry at me.

He opened the middle window, filling the room with cold air.

"Come here, Griet."

I set my rag on the sill and went to him.

"Look out the window."

I looked out. It was a breezy day, with clouds disappearing behind the New Church tower.

"What color are those clouds?"

"Why, white, sir."

He raised his eyebrows slightly. "Are they?"

I glanced at them. "And grey. Perhaps it will snow."

"Come, Griet, you can do better than that. Think of your vegetables."

"My vegetables, sir?"

He moved his head slightly. I was annoying him again. My jaw tightened.

"Think of how you separated the whites. Your turnips and your onions—are they the same white?"

Suddenly I understood. "No. The turnip has green in it, the onion yellow."

"Exactly. Now, what colors do you see in the clouds?"

"There is some blue in them," I said after studying them for a few minutes. "And— yellow as well. And there is some green!" I became so excited I actually pointed. I had been looking at clouds all my life, but I felt as if I saw them for the first time at that moment.

He smiled. "You will find there is little pure white in clouds, yet people say they are white. Now do you understand why I do not need the blue yet?"

"Yes, sir." I did not really understand, but did not want to admit it. I felt I almost knew.

When at last he began to add colors on top of the false colors, I saw what he meant. He painted a light blue over the girl's skirt, and it became a blue through which bits of black could be seen, darker in the shadow of the table, lighter closer to the window. To the wall areas he added yellow ocher, through which some of the grey showed. It became a bright but not a white wall. When the light shone on the wall, I discovered, it was not white, but many colors.

The pitcher and basin were the most complicated—they became yellow, and brown, and green, and blue. They reflected the pattern of the rug, the girl's bodice, the blue cloth draped over the chair—everything but their true silver color. And yet they looked as they should, like a pitcher and a basin.

After that I could not stop looking at things.

❧

It became harder to hide what I was doing when he wanted me to help him make the paints. One morning he took me up to the attic, reached by a ladder in the storeroom next to the studio. I had never been there before. It was a small room, with a steeply slanted roof and a window that let in light and a view of the New Church. There was little there apart from a small cupboard and a stone table with a hollow place in it, holding a stone shaped like an egg with one end cut off. I had seen a similar table once at my father's tile factory. There were also some vessels—basins and shallow earthenware plates—as well as tongs by the tiny fireplace.

"I would like you to grind some things here for me, Griet," he said. He opened a cupboard drawer and took out a black stick the length of my little finger. "This is a piece of ivory, charred in the fire," he explained. "For making black paint."

Dropping it in the bowl of the table, he added a gummy substance that smelled of animal. Then he picked up the stone, which he called a muller, and showed me how to hold it, and how to lean over the table and use my weight against the stone to crush the bone. After a few minutes he had ground it into a fine paste.

"Now you try." He scooped the black paste into a small pot and got out another piece of ivory. I took up the muller and tried to imitate his stance as I leaned over the table.

"No, your hand needs to do this." He placed his hand over mine. The shock of his touch made me drop the muller, which rolled off the table and fell on the floor.

I jumped away from him and bent down to pick it up. "I'm sorry, sir," I muttered, placing the muller in the bowl.

He did not try to touch me again.

"Move your hand up a little," he commanded instead. "That's right. Now use your shoulder to turn, your wrist to finish."

It took me much longer to grind my piece, for I was clumsy and flustered from his touch. And I was smaller than him, and unused to the movement I was meant to make. At least my arms were strong from wringing out laundry.

"A little finer," he suggested when he inspected the bowl. I ground for a few more minutes before he decided it was ready, having me rub the paste between my fingers so I would know how fine he wanted it. Then he laid several more pieces of bone on the table. "Tomorrow I will show you how to grind white lead. It is much easier than bone."

I stared at the ivory.

"What is it, Griet? You're not frightened of a few bones, are you? They are no different from the ivory comb you use to tidy your hair."

I would never be rich enough to own such a comb. I tidied my hair with my fingers.

"It's not that, sir." All the other things he had asked of me I was able to do while cleaning or running errands. No one but Cornelia had become suspicious. But grinding things would take time—I could not do it while I was meant to be cleaning the studio, and I could not explain to others why I must go to the attic at times, leaving my other tasks. "This will take some time to grind," I said feebly.

"Once you are used to it, it will not take as long as today."

I hated to question or disobey him—he was my master. But I feared the anger of the women downstairs. "I'm meant to go to the butcher's now, and to do the ironing, sir. For the mistress." My words sounded petty.

He did not move. "To the butcher's?" He was frowning.

"Yes, sir. The mistress will want to know why I cannot do my other work. She will want to know that I am helping you, up here. It's not easy for me to come up for no reason."

There was a long silence. The bell in the New Church tower struck seven times.

"I see," he murmured when it had stopped. "Let me consider this." He removed some of the ivory, putting it back in a drawer. "Do this bit now." He gestured at what was left. "It shouldn't take long. I must go out. Leave it here when you are done."

He would have to speak to Catharina and tell her about my work. Then it would be easier for me to do things for him.

I waited, but he said nothing to Catharina.

The solution to the problem of the colors came unexpectedly from Tanneke. Since Franciscus' birth the nurse had been sleeping in the Crucifixion room with Tanneke. From there she could get easily to the great hall to feed the baby when he woke. Although Catharina was not feeding him herself, she insisted that Franciscus sleep in a cradle next to her.

I thought this a strange arrangement, but when I came to know Catharina better I understood that she wanted to hold on to the appearance of motherhood, if not the tasks themselves.

Tanneke was not happy sharing her room with the nurse, complaining that the nurse got up too often to tend to the baby, and when she did remain in bed she snored. Tanneke spoke of it to everyone, whether they listened or not. She began to slacken her work, and blamed it on not getting enough sleep. Maria Thins told her there was nothing they could do, but Tanneke continued to grumble. She often threw black looks at me—before I came to live in the house Tanneke had slept where I did in the cellar whenever a nurse was needed. It was almost as if she blamed me for the nurse's snores.

One evening she even appealed to Catharina. Catharina was preparing herself for an evening at the van Ruijvens', despite the cold. She was in a good mood—wearing her pearls and yellow mantle always made her happy. Over her mantle she had tied a wide linen collar that covered her shoulders and protected the cloth from the powder she was dusting on her face. As Tanneke listed her woes, Catharina continued to powder herself, holding up a mirror to inspect the results. Her hair had been dressed in braids and ribbons, and as long as she kept her happy expression she was very beautiful, the combination of her blond hair and light brown eyes making her look exotic.

At last she waved the powder-brush at Tanneke. "Stop!" she cried with a laugh. "We need the nurse and she must sleep near me. There's no space in the girls' room, but there is in yours, so she is there. There's nothing to be done. Why do you bother me about it?"

"Perhaps there is one thing that may be done," he said. I glanced up from the cupboard where I was searching for an apron for Lisbeth. He was standing in the doorway. Catharina gazed up at her husband in surprise. He rarely showed interest in domestic affairs. "Put a bed up in the attic and let someone sleep there. Griet, perhaps."

"Griet in the attic? Why?" Catharina cried.

"Then Tanneke may sleep in the cellar, as she prefers," he explained mildly.

"But—" Catharina stopped, confused. She seemed to disapprove of the idea but could not say why.

"Oh yes, madam," Tanneke broke in eagerly. "That would certainly help." She glanced at me.

I busied myself refolding the children's clothes, though they were already tidy.

"What about the key to the studio?" Catharina finally found an argument. There was only one entrance to the attic, by the ladder in the studio's storeroom. To get to my bed I would have to pass through the studio, which was kept locked at night. "We can't give a maid the key."

"She won't need a key," he countered. "You may lock the studio door once she has gone to bed. Then in the morning she may clean the studio before you come and unlock the door."

I paused with my folding. I did not like the idea of being locked into my room at night.

Unfortunately this notion seemed to please Catharina. Perhaps she thought locking me away would keep me both safely in one place and out of her sight. "All right, then," she decided. She made most decisions quickly. She turned to Tanneke and me. "Tomorrow you two move a bed to the attic. This is only temporary," she added, "until the nurse is no longer needed."

Temporary as my trips to the butcher and fishmonger were meant to be temporary, I thought.

"Come with me to the studio for a moment," he said. He was looking at her in a way I had begun to recognize—a painter's way.

"Me?" Catharina smiled at her husband. Invitations to his studio were rare. She set down her powder-brush with a flourish and began to remove the wide collar, now covered with dust.

He reached out and grasped her hand. "Leave that."

This was almost as surprising as his suggestion to move me to the attic. As he led Catharina upstairs, Tanneke and I exchanged looks.

The next day the baker's daughter began to wear the wide white collar while modelling for the painting.

Maria Thins was not so easily fooled. When she heard from a gleeful Tanneke about her move to the cellar and mine to the attic she puffed on her pipe and frowned. "You two could just switch"—she pointed at us with the pipe— "so that Griet sleeps with the nurse and you go in the cellar. Then there is no need for anyone to move to the attic."

Tanneke was not listening—she was too full of her victory to notice the logic in her mistress's words.

"Mistress has agreed to it," I said simply.

Maria Thins gave me a long sideways look.

Sleeping in the attic made it easier for me to work there, but I still had little time to do so. I could get up earlier and go to bed later, but sometimes he gave me so much work that I had to find a way to go up in the afternoons, when I normally sat by the fire and sewed. I began to complain of not being able to see my stitching in the dim kitchen, and needing the light of my bright attic room. Or I said my stomach hurt and I wanted to lie down. Maria Thins gave me that same sideways look each time I made an excuse, but did not comment.

I began to get used to lying.

Once he had suggested that I sleep in the attic he left it to me to arrange my duties so that I could work for him. He never helped by lying for me, or asking me if I had time to spare for him. He gave me instructions in the morning and expected them to be done by the next day.

The colors themselves made up for the troubles I had hiding what I was doing. I came to love grinding the things he brought from the apothecary—bones, white lead, madder, massicot—to see how bright and pure I could get the colors. I learned that the finer the materials were ground, the deeper the color. From rough, dull grains madder became a fine bright red powder and, mixed with linseed oil, a sparkling paint. Making it and the other colors was magical.

From him I learned too how to wash substances to rid them of impurities and bring out the true colors. I used a series of shells as shallow bowls, and rinsed and rerinsed colors, sometimes thirty times, to get out the chalk or sand or gravel. It was long and tedious work, but very satisfying to see the color grow cleaner with each wash, and closer to what was needed.

The only color he did not allow me to handle was ultramarine. Lapis lazuli was so expensive, and the process of extracting a pure blue from the stone so difficult, that he worked with it himself.

I grew used to being around him. Sometimes we stood side by side in the small room, me grinding white lead, him washing lapis or burning ochers in the fire. He said little to me. He was a quiet man. I did not speak either. It was peaceful then, with the light coming in through the window. When we were done we poured water from a pitcher over each other's hands and scrubbed ourselves clean.

It was very cold in the attic—although there was the little fire he used for heating linseed oil or burning colors, I did not dare light it unless he wanted me to. Otherwise I would have to explain to Catharina and Maria Thins why peat and wood were disappearing so fast.

I did not mind the cold so much when he was there. When he stood close to me I could feel the warmth of his body.

I was washing a bit of massicot I had just ground one afternoon when I heard Maria Thins' voice in the studio below. He was working on the painting, the baker's daughter sighing occasionally as she stood.

"Are you cold, girl?" Maria Thins asked.

"A little," came the faint reply.

"Why doesn't she have a footwarmer?"

His voice was so low that I didn't hear his answer.

"It won't show in the painting, not by her feet. We don't want her getting sick again."

Again I could not hear what he said.

"Griet can get one for her," Maria Thins suggested. "She should be in the attic, for she's meant to have a stomachache. I'll just find her."

She was quicker than I had thought an old woman could be. By the time I put my foot on the top rung she was halfway up the ladder. I stepped back into the attic. I could not escape her, and there was no time to hide anything.

When Maria Thins climbed into the room,

she quickly took in the shells laid in rows on the table, the jug of water, the apron I wore speckled with yellow from the massicot.

"So this is what you've been up to, eh, girl? I thought as much."

I lowered my eyes. I did not know what to say.

"Stomachache, sore eyes. We are not all idiots around here, you know."

Ask him, I longed to tell her. He is my master. This is his doing.

But she did not call to him. Nor did he appear at the bottom of the ladder to explain.

There was a long silence. Then Maria Thins said, "How long have you been assisting him, girl?"

"A few weeks, madam."

"He's been painting faster these last weeks, I've noticed."

I raised my eyes. Her face was calculating.

"You help him to paint faster, girl," she said in a low voice, "and you'll keep your place here. Not a word to my daughter or Tanneke, now."

"Yes, madam."

She chuckled. "I might have known, clever one that you are. You almost fooled even me. Now, get that poor girl down there a foot-warmer."

I liked sleeping in the attic. There was no Crucifixion scene hanging at the foot of the bed to trouble me. There were no paintings at all, but the clean scent of linseed oil and the musk of the earth pigments. I liked my view of the New Church, and the quiet. No one came up except him. The girls did not visit me as they sometimes had in the cellar, or secretly search through my things. I felt alone there, perched high above the noisy household, able to see it from a distance.

Rather like him.

The best part, however, was that I could spend more time in the studio. Sometimes I wrapped myself in a blanket and crept down late at night when the house was still. I looked at the painting he was working on by candlelight, or opened a shutter a little to let in moonlight. Sometimes I sat in the dark in one of the lion-head chairs pulled up to the table and rested my elbow on the blue and red table rug that covered it. I imagined wearing the yellow and black bodice and pearls, holding a glass of wine, sitting across the table from him.

There was one thing I did not like about the attic, however. I did not like being locked in at night.

Catharina had got the studio key back from Maria Thins and began to lock and unlock the door. She must have felt it gave her some control over me. She was not happy about my being in the attic—it meant I was closer to him, to the place she was not allowed in but where I could wander freely.

It must have been hard for a wife to accept such an arrangement.

It worked for a time, however. For a time I was able to slip away in the afternoons and wash and grind colors for him. Catharina often slept then—Franciscus had not settled, and woke her most nights so that she needed sleep during the day. Tanneke usually fell asleep by the fire as well, and I could leave the kitchen without always having to make up an excuse. The girls were busy with Johannes, teaching him to walk and talk, and rarely noticed my absence. If they did Maria Thins said I was running an errand for her, fetching things from her rooms, or sewing something for her that needed bright attic light to work by. They were children, after all, absorbed in their own world, indifferent to the adult lives around them except when it directly affected them.

Or so I thought.

One afternoon I was washing white lead when Cornelia called my name from downstairs. I quickly wiped my hands, removed the apron I wore for attic work and changed into my daily apron before climbing down the ladder to her. She stood on the threshold of the studio, looking as if she were standing at the edge of a puddle and tempted to step in it.

"What is it?" I spoke rather sharply.

"Tanneke wants you." Cornelia turned and led the way to the stairs. She hesitated at the top. "Will you help me, Griet?" she asked plaintively. "Go first so that if I fall you will catch me. The stairs are so steep."

It was unlike her to be scared, even on

stairs she did not use much. I was touched, or perhaps I was simply feeling guilty for being sharp with her. I descended the stairs, then turned and held out my arms. "Now you."

Cornelia was standing at the top, hands in her pockets. She started down the stairs, one hand on the banister, the other balled into a tight fist. When she was most of the way down she let go and jumped so that she fell against me, sliding down my front, pressing painfully into my stomach. Once she regained her feet she began to laugh, head thrown up, brown eyes narrowed to slits.

"Naughty girl," I muttered, regretting my softness.

I found Tanneke in the cooking kitchen, Johannes in her lap.

"Cornelia said you wanted me."

"Yes, she's torn one of her collars and wants you to mend it. Wouldn't let me touch it—I don't know why, she knows I mend collars best." As Tanneke handed it to me her eyes strayed to my apron. "What's that there? Are you bleeding?"

I looked down. A slash of red dust crossed my stomach like a streak on a window pane. For a moment I thought of the aprons of Pieter the father and son.

Tanneke leaned closer. "That's not blood. It looks like powder. How did that get there?"

I gazed at the streak. Madder, I thought. I ground this a few weeks ago.

Only I heard the stifled giggle from the hallway.

Cornelia had been waiting some time for this mischief. She had even managed somehow to get up to the attic to steal the powder.

I did not make up an answer fast enough. As I hesitated, Tanneke's suspicion grew. "Have you been in the master's things?" she said in an accusing tone. She had, after all, modelled for him and knew what he kept in the studio.

"No, it was—" I stopped. If I tattled on Cornelia I would sound petty and it would probably not stop Tanneke from discovering what I did in the.attic.

"I think young mistress had better see this," she decided.

"No," I said quickly.

Tanneke drew herself up as much as she could with a sleeping child in her lap. "Take off your apron," she commanded, "so I can show it to the young mistress."

"Tanneke," I said, gazing levelly at her, "if you know what's best for you, you'll not disturb Catharina, you'll speak to Maria Thins. Alone, not in front of the girls."

It was those words, with their bullying tone, that caused the most damage between Tanneke and me. I did not think to sound like that—I was simply desperate to stop her from telling Catharina any way I could. But she would never forgive me for treating her as if she were below me.

My words at least had their effect. Tanneke gave me a hard, angry look, but behind it was uncertainty, and the desire indeed to tell her own beloved mistress. She hung between that desire and the wish to punish my impudence by disobeying me.

"Speak to your mistress," I said softly. "But speak to her alone."

Though my back was to the door, I sensed Cornelia slipping away from it.

Tanneke's own instincts won. With a stony face she handed Johannes to me and went to find Maria Thins. Before I settled him on my lap I carefully wiped away the red pigment with a rag, then threw it in the fire. It still left a stain. I sat with my arms around the little boy and waited for my fate to be decided.

I never found out what Maria Thins said to Tanneke, what threats or promises she made to keep her quiet. But it worked—Tanneke said nothing about my attic work to Catharina or the girls, or to me. She became much harder with me, though—deliberately difficult rather than unthinkingly so. She sent me back to the fish stalls with the cod I knew she had asked for, swearing she had told me to buy flounder. When she cooked she became sloppier, spilling as much grease as she could on her apron so that I would have to soak the cloth longer and scrub harder to get the grease out. She left buckets for me to empty, and stopped bringing water to fill the kitchen cistern or mopping the floors. She sat and watched me balefully, refusing to move her feet so that I had to mop around them, to find afterwards that one foot had covered a sticky puddle of grease.

She did not talk kindly to me any longer. She

made me feel alone in a house full of people.

So I did not dare to take nice things from her kitchen to cheer my father with. And I did not tell my parents how hard things were for me at the Oude Langendijck, how careful I had to be to keep my place. Nor could I tell them about the few good things—the colors I made, the nights when I sat alone in the studio, the moments when he and I worked side by side and I was warmed by his presence.

All I could tell them about were his paintings.

One April morning when the cold at last had gone, I was walking along the Koornmarkt to the apothecary when Pieter the son appeared at my side and wished me good day. I had not seen him earlier. He wore a clean apron and carried a bundle, which he said he was delivering further along the Koornmarkt. He was going the same way as me and asked if he could walk with me. I nodded—I did not feel I could say no. Through the winter I had seen him once or twice a week at the Meat Hall. I always found it hard to meet his gaze—his eyes felt like needles pricking my skin. His attention worried me.

"You look tired," he said now. "Your eyes are red. They are working you too hard."

Indeed, they were working me hard. My master had given me so much bone to grind that I had to get up very early to finish it. And the night before Tanneke had made me stay up late to rewash the kitchen floor after she spilled a pan of grease all over it.

I did not want to blame my master. "Tanneke has taken against me," I said instead, "and gives me more to do. Then, of course, it's getting warmer as well and we are cleaning the winter out of the house." I added this so that he would not think I was complaining about her.

"Tanneke is an odd one," he said, "but loyal."

"To Maria Thins, yes."

"To the family as well. Remember how she defended Catharina from her mad brother?"

I shook my head. "I don't know what you mean."

Pieter looked surprised. "It was the talk of the Meat Hall for days. Ah, but you don't gossip, do you? You keep your eyes open but you don't tell tales, or listen to them." He seemed to approve. "Me, I hear it all day from the old ones waiting for meat. Can't help but some of it sticks."

"What did Tanneke do?" I asked despite myself.

Pieter smiled. "When your mistress was carrying the last child but one—what's its name?"

"Johannes. Like his father."

Pieter's smile dimmed like a cloud crossing the sun. "Yes, like his father." He took up the tale again. "One day Catharina's brother, Willem, came around to the Oude Lan-

141

gendijck, when she was big with child, and began to beat her, right in the street."

"Why?"

"He's missing a brick or two, they say. He's always been violent. His father as well. You know the father and Maria Thins separated many years ago? He used to beat her."

"Beat Maria Thins?" I repeated in wonder. I would never have guessed that anyone could beat Maria Thins.

"So when Willem began hitting Catharina it seems Tanneke got in between them to protect her. Even thumped him soundly."

Where was my master when this happened? I thought. He could not have remained in his studio. He could not have. He must have been out at the Guild, or with van Leeuwenhoek, or at Mechelen, his mother's inn.

"Maria Thins and Catharina managed to have Willem confined last year," Pieter continued. "Can't leave the house he's lodged in. That's why you haven't seen him. Have you really heard nothing of this? Don't they talk in your house?"

"Not to me." I thought of all the times Catharina and her mother put their heads together in the Crucifixion room, falling silent when I entered. "And I don't listen behind door-ways."

"Of course you don't." Pieter was smiling again as if I had told a joke. Like everyone else, he thought all maids eavesdropped. There were many assumptions about maids that people made about me.

142

I was silent the rest of the way. I had not known that Tanneke could be so loyal and brave, despite all she said behind Catharina's back, or that Catharina had suffered such blows, or that Maria Thins could have such a son. I tried to imagine my own brother beating me in the street but could not.

Pieter said no more—he could see my confusion. When he left me in front of the apothecary he simply touched my elbow and continued on his way. I had to stand for a moment looking into the dark green water of the canal before I shook my head to clear it and turned to the apothecary's door.

I was shaking from my thoughts a picture of the knife spinning on my mother's kitchen floor.

One Sunday Pieter the son came to services at our church. He must have slipped in after my parents and me, and sat in the back, for I did not see him until afterward when we were outside speaking to our neighbors. He was standing off to one side, watching me. When I caught sight of him I drew in my breath sharply. At least, I thought, he is Protestant. I had not been certain before. Since working in the house at Papists' Corner I was no longer certain of many things.

My mother followed my gaze. "Who is that?"

"The butcher's son."

She gave me a curious look, part surprise, part fear. "Go to him," she whispered, "and bring him to us."

I obeyed her and went up to Pieter. "Why are you here?" I asked, knowing I should be more polite.

He smiled. "Hello, Griet. No pleasant words for me?"

"Why are you here?"

"I'm going to services in every church in Delft, to see which I like best. It may take some time." When he saw my face he dropped his tone—joking was not the way with me. "I came to see you, and to meet your parents."

I blushed so hot I felt feverish. "I would rather you did not," I said softly.

"Why not?"

"I'm only seventeen. I don't—I'm not thinking of such things yet."

"There's no rush," Pieter said.

I looked down at his hands—they were clean, but there were still traces of blood around his nails. I thought of my master's hand over mine as he showed me how to grind bone, and shivered.

People were staring at us, for he was a stranger to the church. And he was a handsome man—even I could see that, with his long blond curls, bright eyes and ready smile. Several young women were trying to catch his eye.

"Will you introduce me to your parents?"

Reluctantly I led him to them. Pieter nodded to my mother and grasped my father's hand, who stepped back nervously. Since he had lost

144

his eyes he was shy of meeting strangers. And he had never before met a man who showed interest in me.

"Don't worry, Father," I whispered to him while my mother was introducing Pieter to a neighbor, "you aren't losing me."

"We've already lost you, Griet. We lost you the moment you became a maid."

I was glad he could not see the tears that pricked my eyes.

Pieter the son did not come every week to our church, but he came often enough that each Sunday I grew nervous, smoothing my skirt more than it needed, pressing my lips together as we sat in our pew.

"Has he come? Is he here?" my father would ask each Sunday, turning his head this way and that.

I let my mother answer. "Yes," she would say, "he is here," or "No, he has not come."

Pieter always said hello to my parents before greeting me. At first they were uneasy with him. However, Pieter chatted easily to them, ignoring their awkward responses and long silences. He knew how to talk to people, meeting so many at his father's stall. After several Sundays my parents became used to him. The first time my father laughed at something Pieter said he was so surprised at himself that he immediately frowned, until Pieter said something else to make him laugh again.

There was always a moment after they had been speaking when my parents stepped back and left us alone. Pieter wisely let them decide when. The first few times it did not happen at all. Then one Sunday my mother pointedly took my father's arm and said, "Let us go and speak to the minister."

For several Sundays I dreaded that moment until I too became used to being on my own with him in front of so many watchful eyes. Pieter sometimes teased me gently, but more often he asked me what I had been doing during the week, or told me stories he had heard in the Meat Hall, or described auctions at the Beast Market. He was patient with me when I became tongue-tied or sharp or dismissive.

He never asked me about my master. I never told him I was working with the colors. I was glad he did not ask me.

On those Sundays I felt very confused. When I should be listening to Pieter I found myself thinking about my master.

One Sunday in May, when I had been working at the house on the Oude Langendijck for almost a year, my mother said to Pieter just before she and my father left us alone, "Will you come back to eat with us after next Sunday's service?"

Pieter smiled as I gaped at her. "I'll come."

I barely heard what he said after that. When he finally left and my parents and I went home I had to bite my lips so that I would not shout. "Why didn't you tell me you were going to invite Pieter?" I muttered.

My mother glanced at me sideways. "It's time we asked him," was all she said.

She was right—it would be rude of us not to invite him to our house. I had not played this game with a man before, but I had seen what went on with others. If Pieter was serious, then my parents would have to treat him seriously.

I also knew what a hardship it would be to them to have him come. My parents had very little now. Despite my wages and what my mother made from spinning wool for others, they could barely feed themselves, much less another mouth—and a butcher's mouth at that. I could do little to help them—take what I could from Tanneke's kitchen, a bit of wood, perhaps, some onions, some bread. They would eat less that week and light the fire less, just so that they could feed him properly.

But they insisted that he come. They would not say so to me, but they must have seen feeding him as a way of filling our own stomachs in the future. A butcher's wife—and her parents—would always eat well. A little hunger now would bring a heavy stomach eventually.

Later, when he began coming regularly, Pieter sent them gifts of meat which my mother would cook for the Sunday. At that first Sunday dinner, however, she sensibly did not serve meat to a butcher's son. He would have been able to judge exactly how poor they were by the cut of the joint. Instead she made a fish stew, even adding shrimps and lobster, never telling me how she managed to pay for them.

The house, though shabby, gleamed from her attentions. She had got out some of my father's best tiles, those she had not had to sell, and polished and lined them up along the wall so Peter could look at them as he ate. He praised my mother's stew, and his words were genuine. She was pleased, and blushed and smiled and gave him more. Afterwards he asked my father about the tiles, describing each one until my father recognized it and could complete the description.

"Griet has the best one," he said after they had gone through all those in the room. "It's of her and her brother."

"I'd like to see it," Pieter murmured.

I studied my chapped hands in my lap and swallowed. I had not told them what Cornelia had done to my tile.

As Pieter was leaving my mother whispered to me to see him to the end of the street. I walked beside him, sure that our neighbors were staring, though in truth it was a rainy day and there were few people out. I felt as if my parents had pushed me into the street, that a deal had been made and I was being passed into the hands of a man. At least he is a good man, I thought, even if his hands are not as clean as they could be.

Close to the Rietveld Canal there was an alley that Pieter guided me to, his hand at the small of my back. Agnes used to hide there during our games as children. I stood against the wall and let Pieter kiss me. He was so eager that he bit my lips. I did not cry out—I licked away the salty blood and looked over his shoulder at the wet brick wall opposite as he pushed himself against me. A raindrop fell into my eye.

I would not let him do all he wanted. After a time Pieter stepped back. He reached a hand towards my head. I moved away.

"You favor your caps, don't you?" he said.

"I'm not rich enough to dress my hair and go without a cap," I snapped. "Nor am I a—" I did not finish. I did not need to tell him what other kind of woman left her head bare.

"But your cap covers all your hair. Why is that? Most women show some of their hair."

I did not answer.

"What color is your hair?"

"Brown."

"Light or dark?"

"Dark."

Pieter smiled as if he were indulging a child in a game. "Straight or curly?"

"Neither. Both." I winced at my confusion.

"Long or short?"

I hesitated. "Below my shoulders."

He continued to smile at me, then kissed me once more and turned back toward Market Square.

I had hesitated because I did not want to lie but did not want him to know. My hair was long and could not be tamed. When it was uncovered it seemed to belong to another Griet—a Griet who would stand in an alley alone with a man, who was not so calm and quiet and clean. A Griet like the women who dared to bare their heads. That was why I kept my hair completely hidden—so that there would be no trace of that Griet.

He finished the painting of the baker's daughter. This time I had warning, for he stopped asking me to grind and wash colors. He did not use much paint now, nor did he make sudden changes at the end as he had with the woman with the pearl necklace. He had made changes earlier, removing one of the chairs from the painting, and moving the map along the wall. I was less surprised by such changes, for I'd had the chance to think of them myself, and knew that what he did made the painting better.

He borrowed van Leeuwenhoek's camera obscura again to look at the scene one last time. When he had set it up he allowed me to look through it as well. Although I still did not understand how it worked, I came to admire the scenes the camera painted inside itself, the miniature, reversed pictures of things in the room. The colors of ordinary objects became more intense—the table rug a deeper red, the wall map a glowing brown like a glass of ale held up to the sun. I was not sure how the camera helped him to paint, but I was becoming more like Maria Thins—if it made him paint better, I did not question it.

He was not painting faster, however. He spent five months on the girl with the water pitcher. I often worried that Maria Thins would remind me that I had not helped him to work faster, and tell me to pack my things and leave.

She did not. She knew that he had been very busy at the Guild that winter, as well as at Mechelen. Perhaps she had decided to wait and see if things would change in the summer. Or perhaps she found it hard to chide him since she liked the painting so much.

"It's a shame such a fine painting is to go only to the baker," she said one day. "We could have charged more if it were for van Ruijven." It was clear that while he painted the works, it was she who struck the deals.

The baker liked the painting too. The day he came to see it was very different from the formal visit van Ruijven and his wife had made several months before to view their painting. The baker brought his whole family, including several children and a sister or two. He was a merry man, with a face permanently flushed from the heat of his ovens and hair that looked as if it had been dipped in flour. He refused the wine Maria Thins offered, preferring a mug of beer. He loved children, and insisted that the four girls and Johannes be allowed into the studio. They loved him as well—each time he visited he brought them another shell for their collection. This time it was a conch as big as my hand, rough and spiky and white with pale yellow marks on the outside, a polished pink and orange on the inside. The girls were delighted, and ran to get their other shells. They brought them upstairs and they and the baker's children played together in the storeroom while Tanneke and I served the guests in the studio.

The baker announced he was satisfied with the painting. "My daughter looks well, and that's enough for me," he said.

Afterwards, Maria Thins lamented that he had not looked at it as closely as van Ruijven would have, that his senses were dulled by the beer he drank and the disorder he surrounded himself with. I did not agree, though I did not say so. It seemed to me that the baker had an honest response to the painting. Van Ruijven tried too hard when he looked at paintings, with his honeyed words and studied expressions. He was too aware of having an audience to perform for, whereas the baker merely said what he thought.

I checked on the children in the storeroom. They had spread across the floor, sorting shells and getting sand everywhere. The chests and books and dishes and cushions kept there did not interest them.

Cornelia was climbing down the ladder from the attic. She jumped from three rungs up and shouted triumphantly as she crashed to the floor. When she looked at me briefly, her eyes were a challenge. One of the baker's sons, about Aleydis' age, climbed partway up the ladder and jumped to the floor. Then

Aleydis tried it, and another child, and another.

I had never known how Cornelia managed to get to the attic to steal the madder that stained my apron red. It was in her nature to be sly, to slip away when no one was looking. I had said nothing to Maria Thins or him about her pilfering. I was not sure they would believe me. Instead I had made sure the colors were locked away whenever he and I were not there.

I said nothing to her now as she sprawled on the floor next to Maertge. But that night I checked my things. Everything was there— my broken tile, my tortoiseshell comb, my prayer book, my embroidered handkerchiefs, my collars, my chemises, my aprons and caps. I counted and sorted and refolded them.

Then I checked the colors, just to be sure. They too were in order, and the cupboard did not look as if it had been tampered with.

Perhaps she was just being a child after all, climbing a ladder to jump from it, looking for a game rather than mischief.

The baker took away his painting in May, but my master did not begin setting up the next painting until July. I grew anxious about this delay, expecting Maria Thins to blame me, even though we both knew that it was not my fault. Then one day I overheard her tell Catharina that a friend of van Ruijven's saw the painting of his wife with the pearl necklace and thought she should be looking out rather than at a mirror. Van Ruijven had thus decided that he wanted a painting with his wife's face turned towards the painter. "He doesn't paint that pose often," she remarked.

I could not hear Catharina's response. I stopped sweeping the floor of the girls' room for a moment.

"You remember the last one," Maria Thins reminded her. "The maid. Remember van Ruijven and the maid in the red dress?"

Catharina snorted with muffled laughter.

"That was the last time anyone looked out from one of his paintings," Maria Thins continued, "and what a scandal that was! I was sure he would say no when van Ruijven suggested it this time, but he has agreed to do it."

I could not ask Maria Thins, who would know I had been listening to them. I could not ask Tanneke, who would never repeat gossip to me now. So one day when there were few people at his stall I asked Pieter the son if he had heard about the maid in the red dress.

"Oh yes, that story went all around the Meat Hall," he answered, chuckling. He leaned over and began rearranging the cows' tongues on display. "It was several years ago now. It seems van Ruijven wanted one of his kitchen maids to sit for a painting with him. They dressed her in one of his wife's gowns, a red one, and van Ruijven made sure there was wine in the painting so he could get her to drink every time they sat together. Sure enough, before the painting was finished she was carrying van Ruijven's child."

"What happened to her?"

Pieter shrugged. "What happens to girls like that?"

His words froze my blood. Of course I had heard such stories before, but never one so close to me. I thought about my dreams of wearing Catharina's clothes, of van Ruijven grasping my chin in the hallway, of him saying "You should paint her" to my master.

Pieter had stopped what he was doing, a frown on his face. "Why do you want to know about her?"

"It's nothing," I answered lightly. "Just something I overheard. It means nothing."

I had not been present when he set up the scene for the painting of the baker's daughter—I had not yet been assisting him. Now, however, the first time van Ruijven's wife came to sit for him I was up in the attic working, and could hear what he said. She was a quiet woman. She did what was asked of her without a sound. Even her fine shoes did not tap across the tiled floor. He had her stand by the unshuttered window, then sit in one of the two lion-head chairs placed around the table. I heard him close some shutters. "This painting will be darker than the last," he declared.

She did not respond. It was as if he were talking to himself. After a moment he called up to me. When I appeared he said, "Griet get my wife's yellow mantle, and her pearl necklace and earrings."

Catharina was visiting friends that afternoon so I could not ask her for her jewels. I would have been frightened to anyway. Instead I went to Maria Thins in the Crucifixion room, who unlocked Catharina's jewelry box and handed me the necklace and earrings. Then I got out the mantle from the cupboard in the great hall, shook it out and folded it carefully over my arm. I had never touched it before. I let my nose sink into the fur—it was very soft, like a baby rabbit's.

As I walked down the hallway to the stairs I had the sudden desire to run out the door with the riches in my arms. I could go to the star in the middle of Market Square, choose a direction to follow, and never come back.

Instead I returned to van Ruijven's wife and helped her into the mantle. She wore it as if it were her own skin. After sliding the earring wires through the holes in her lobes, she looped the pearls around her neck. I had taken up the ribbons to tie the necklace for her when he said, "Don't wear the necklace. Leave it on the table."

She sat again. He sat in his chair and studied her. She did not seem to mind—she gazed into space, seeing nothing, as he had tried to get me to do.

"Look at me," he said.

She looked at him. Her eyes were large and dark, almost black.

He laid a table rug on the table, then changed it for the blue cloth. He laid the pearls in a line on the table, then in a heap, then in a line again. He asked her to stand, to sit, then to sit back, then to sit forward.

I thought he had forgotten that I was watching from the corner until he said, "Griet, get me Catharina's powder-brush."

He had her hold the brush up to her face, lay it on the table with her hand still grasping it, leave it to one side. He handed it to me. "Take it back."

When I returned he had given her a quill and paper. She sat in the chair, leaning forward, and wrote, an inkwell at her right. He opened a pair of the upper shutters and closed the bottom pair. The room became darker but the light shone on her high round forehead, on her arm resting on the table, on the sleeve of the yellow mantle.

"Move your left hand forward slightly," he said. "There."

She wrote.

"Look at me," he said.

She looked at him.

He got a map from the storeroom and hung it on the wall behind her. He took it down again. He tried a small landscape, a painting of a ship, the bare wall. Then he disappeared downstairs.

While he was gone I watched van Ruijven's wife closely. It was perhaps rude of me, but I wanted to see what she would do. She did not move. She seemed to settle into the pose more completely. By the time he returned, with a still life of musical instruments, she looked as if she had always been sitting at the table, writing her letter. I had heard he painted her once before the previous necklace painting, playing a lute. She must have learned by now what he wanted from a model. Perhaps she simply was what he wanted.

He hung the painting behind her, then sat down again to study her. As they gazed at each other I felt as if I were not there. I wanted to leave, to go back to my colors, but I did not dare disturb the moment.

"The next time you come, wear white ribbons in your hair instead of pink, and a yellow ribbon where you tie your hair at the back."

She nodded so slightly that her head hardly moved.

"You may sit back."

As he released her, I felt free to go.

The next day he pulled up another chair to the table. The day after that he brought up Catharina's jewelry box and set it on the table. Its drawers were studded with pearls around the keyholes.

Van Leeuwenhoek arrived with his camera obscura while I was working in the attic. "You will have to get one of your own some day," I heard him say in his deep voice. "Though I admit it gives me the opportunity to see what you're painting. Where is the model?"

"She could not come."

"That is a problem."

"No. Griet," he called.

I climbed down the ladder. When I entered the studio van Leeuwenhoek gazed at me in astonishment. He had very clear brown eyes, with large lids that made him look sleepy. He was far from sleepy, though, but alert and puzzled, his mouth drawn in tightly at the corners. Despite his surprise at seeing me, he had a kindly look about him, and when he recovered he even bowed.

No gentleman had ever bowed to me before. I could not stop myself—I smiled.

Van Leeuwenhoek laughed. "What were you doing up there, my dear?"

"Grinding colors, sir."

He turned to my master. "An assistant! What other surprises do you have for me? Next you'll be teaching her to paint your women for you."

My master was not amused. "Griet," he said, "sit as you saw van Ruijven's wife do the other day."

I stepped nervously to the chair and sat, leaning forward as she had done.

"Take up the quill."

I picked it up, my hand trembling and making the feather shake, and placed my hands as I had remembered hers. I prayed he would not ask me to write something, as he had van Ruijven's wife. My father had taught me to write my name, but little else. At least I knew how to hold the quill. I glanced at the sheets on the table and wondered what van Ruijven's wife had written on them. I could read a little, from familiar things like my prayer book, but not a lady's hand.

"Look at me."

I looked at him. I tried to be van Ruijven's wife.

He cleared his throat. "She will be wearing the yellow mantle," he said to van Leeuwenhoek, who nodded.

My master stood, and they set up the camera obscura so that it pointed at me. Then they took turns looking. When they were bent over the box with the black robe over their heads, it became easier for me to sit and think of nothing, as I knew he wanted me to.

He had van Leeuwenhoek move the painting on the back wall several times before he was satisfied with its position, then open and shut shutters while he kept his head under the robe. At last he seemed satisfied. He stood up and folded the robe over the back of the chair, then stepped over to the desk, picked up a piece of paper, and handed it to van Leeuwenhoek. They began discussing its contents—Guild business he wanted advice about. They talked for a long time.

Van Leeuwenhoek glanced up. "For the mercy of God, man, let the girl get back to her work."

My master looked at me as if surprised that I was still sitting at the table, quill in hand. "Griet, you may go."

As I left I thought I saw a look of pity cross van Leeuwenhoek's face.

He left the camera set up in the studio for some days. I was able to look through it several times on my own, lingering on the objects on the table. Something about the scene he was to paint bothered me. It was like looking at a painting that has been hung crookedly. I wanted to change something, but I did not know what. The box gave me no answers.

One day van Ruijven's wife came again and he looked at her for a long time in the camera. I was passing through the studio while his head was covered, and walked as quietly as I could so I would not disturb them. I stood behind him for a moment to look at the setting with her in it. She must have seen me but gave no sign, continuing to gaze straight at him with her dark eyes.

It came to me then that the scene was too neat. Although I valued tidiness over most things, I knew from his other paintings that there should be some disorder on the table, something to snag the eye. I pondered each object—the jewelry box, the blue table rug, the pearls, the letter, the inkwell—and decided what I would change. I returned quietly to the attic, surprised by my bold thoughts.

Once it was clear to me what he should do to the scene, I waited for him to make the change.

He did not move anything on the table. He adjusted the shutters slightly, the tilt of her head, the angle of her quill. But he did not change what I had expected him to.

I thought about it while I was wringing out sheets, while I was turning the spit for Tanneke, while I was wiping the kitchen tiles, while I was rinsing colors. While I lay in bed at night I thought about it. Sometimes I got up to look again. No, I was not mistaken.

He returned the camera to van Leeuwenhoek.

Whenever I looked at the scene my chest grew tight as if something were pressing on it.

He set a canvas on the easel and painted a coat of lead white and chalk mixed with a bit of burnt sienna and yellow ocher.

My chest grew tighter, waiting for him.

He sketched lightly in reddish brown the outline of the woman and of each object.

When he began to paint great blocks of false colors, I thought my chest would burst like a sack that has been filled with too much flour.

As I lay in bed one night I decided I would have to make the change myself.

The next morning I cleaned, setting the jewelry box back carefully, relining the pearls, replacing the letter, polishing and replacing the inkwell. I took a deep breath to ease the pressure in my chest. Then in one quick movement I pulled the front part of the blue cloth onto the table so that it flowed out of the dark shadows under the table and up in a slant onto the table in front of the jewelry box. I made a few adjustments to the lines of the folds, then stepped back. It echoed the shape of van Ruijven's wife's arm as she held the quill.

Yes, I thought, and pressed my lips together.

162

He may send me away for changing it, but it is better now.

That afternoon I did not go up to the attic, although there was plenty of work for me there. I sat outside on the bench with Tanneke and mended shirts. He had not gone to his studio that morning, but to the Guild, and had dined at van Leeuwenhoek's. He had not yet seen the change.

I waited anxiously on the bench. Even Tanneke, who tried to ignore me these days, noted my mood. "What's the matter with you, girl?" she asked. She had taken to calling me girl like her mistress. "You're acting like a chicken that knows it's for the slaughter."

"Nothing," I said. "Tell me about what happened when Catharina's brother came here last. I heard about it at the market. They still mention you," I added, hoping to distract and flatter her, and to cover up how clumsily I moved away from her question.

For a moment Tanneke sat up straighter, until she remembered who was asking. "That's not your business," she snapped. "That's family business, not for the likes of you."

A few months before she would have delighted in telling a story that set her in the best light. But it was me who was asking, and I was not to be trusted or humored or favored with her words, though it must have pained her to pass up the chance to boast.

Then I saw him—he was walking towards us up the Oude Langendijck, his hat tilted to shield his face from the spring sunlight, his dark cloak pushed back from his shoulders. As he drew up to us I could not look at him.

"Afternoon, sir," Tanneke sang out in a completely different tone.

"Hello, Tanneke. Are you enjoying the sun?"

"Oh yes, sir. I do like the sun on my face."

I kept my eyes on the stitches I had made. I could feel him looking at me.

After he went inside Tanneke hissed, "Say hello to the master when he speaks to you, girl. Your manners are a disgrace."

"It was you he spoke to."

"And so he should. But you needn't be so rude or you'll end up in the street, with no place here."

He must be upstairs now, I thought. He must have seen what I've done.

I waited, barely able to hold my needle. I did not know exactly what I expected. Would he berate me in front of Tanneke? Would he raise his voice for the first time since I had come to live in his house? Would he say the painting was ruined?

Perhaps he would simply pull down the blue cloth so that it hung as it had before. Perhaps he would say nothing to me.

Later that night I saw him briefly as he came down for supper. He did not appear to be one thing or the other, happy or angry, unconcerned or anxious. He did not ignore me but he did not look at me either.

When I went up to bed I checked to see if he had pulled the cloth to hang as it had before I touched it.

He had not. I held up my candle to the easel—he had resketched in reddish brown the folds of the blue cloth. He had made my change.

I lay in bed that night smiling in the dark.

The next morning he came in as I was cleaning around the jewelry box. He had never before seen me making my measurements. I had laid my arm along one edge and moved the box to dust under and around it. When I looked over he was watching me. He did not say anything. Nor did I—I was concerned to set the box back exactly as it had been. Then I sponged the blue cloth with a damp rag, especially careful with the new folds I had made. My hands shook a little as I cleaned.

When I was done I looked up at him.

"Tell me, Griet, why did you change the tablecloth?" His tone was the same as when he had asked me about the vegetables at my parents' house.

I thought for a moment. "There needs to be some disorder in the scene, to contrast with her tranquillity," I explained. "Something to tease the eye. And yet it must be something pleasing to the eye as well, and it is, because the cloth and her arm are in a similar position."

There was a long pause. He was gazing at the table. I waited, wiping my hands against my apron.

"I had not thought I would learn something from a maid," he said at last.

On Sunday my mother joined us as I described the new painting to my father. Pieter was with us, and had fixed his eyes on a patch of sunlight on the floor. He was always quiet when we talked about my master's paintings.

I did not tell them about the change I had made that my master approved of.

"I think his paintings are not good for the soul," my mother announced suddenly. She was frowning. She had never before spoken of his work.

My father turned his face towards her in surprise.

"Good for the purse, more like," Frans quipped. It was one of the rare Sundays when he was visiting. Lately he had become obsessed with money. He questioned me about the value of things in the house on the Oude Langendijck, of the pearls and mantle in the painting, of the pearl-encrusted jewelry box and what it held, of the number and size of paintings that hung on the walls. I did not tell him much. I was sorry to think it of my own brother, but I feared his thoughts had turned to easier ways of making a living than as an apprentice in a tile factory. I suspected he was only dreaming, but I did not want to fuel those dreams with visions of expensive objects within his—or his sister's—reach.

"What do you mean, Mother?" I asked, ignoring Frans.

"There is something dangerous about your

description of his paintings," she explained. "From the way you talk they could be of religious scenes. It is as if the woman you describe is the Virgin Mary when she is just a woman, writing a letter. You give the painting meaning that it does not have or deserve. There are thousands of paintings in Delft. You can see them everywhere, hanging in a tavern as readily as in a rich man's house. You could take two weeks' maid's wages and buy one at the market."

"If I did that," I replied, "you and Father would not eat for two weeks, and you would die without seeing what I bought."

My father winced. Frans, who had been tying knots in a length of string, went very still. Pieter glanced at me.

My mother remained impassive. She did not speak her mind often. When she did her words were worth gold.

"I'm sorry, Mother," I stammered. "I didn't mean—"

"Working for them has turned your head," she interrupted. "It's made you forget who you are and where you come from. We're a decent Protestant family whose needs are not ruled by riches or fashions."

I looked down, stung by her words. They were a mother's words, words I would say to my own daughter if I were concerned for her. Although I resented her speaking them, as I resented her questioning the value of his painting, I knew they held truth.

Pieter did not spend so long with me in the alley that Sunday.

The next morning it was painful to look at the painting. The blocks of false colors had been painted, and he had built up her eyes, and the high dome of her forehead, and part of the folds of the mantle sleeve. The rich yellow in particular filled me with the guilty pleasure that my mother's words had condemned. I tried instead to picture the finished painting hanging at Pieter the father's stall, for sale for ten guilders, a simple picture of a woman writing a letter.

I could not do it.

He was in a good mood that afternoon, or else I would not have asked him. I had learned to gauge his mood, not from the little he said or the expression on his face—he did not show much—but from the way he moved about the studio and attic. When he was happy, when he was working well, he strode purposefully back and forth, no hesitation in his stride, no movement wasted. If he had been a musical man, he would have been humming or singing or whistling under his breath. When things did not go well, he stopped, stared out the window, shifted abruptly, started up the attic ladder only to climb back down before he was halfway up.

"Sir," I began when he came up to the attic to mix linseed oil into the white lead I had finished grinding. He was working on the fur of the sleeve. She had not come that day, but I had discovered he was able to paint parts of her without her being there.

He raised his eyebrows. "Yes, Griet?"

He and Maertge were the only people in the house who always called me by my name.

"Are your paintings Catholic paintings?"

He paused, the bottle of linseed oil poised over the shell that held the white lead. "Catholic paintings," he repeated. He lowered his hand, tapping the bottle against the table top. "What do you mean by a Catholic painting?"

I had spoken before thinking. Now I did not know what to say. I tried a different question. "Why are there paintings in Catholic churches?"

"Have you ever been inside a Catholic church, Griet?"

"No, sir."

"Then you have not seen paintings in a church, or statues or stained glass?"

"No."

"You have seen paintings only in houses, or shops, or inns?"

"And at the market."

"Yes, at the market. Do you like looking at paintings?"

"I do, sir." I began to think he would not answer me, that he would simply ask me endless questions.

"What do you see when you look at one?"

"Why, what the painter has painted, sir."

Although he nodded, I felt I had not answered as he wished.

"So when you look at the painting down in the studio, what do you see?"

"I do not see the Virgin Mary, that is certain." I said this more in defiance of my mother than in answer to him.

He gazed at me in surprise. "Did you expect to see the Virgin Mary?"

"Oh no, sir," I replied, flustered.

"Do you think the painting is Catholic?"

"I don't know, sir. My mother said—"

"Your mother has not seen the painting, has she?"

"No."

"Then she cannot tell you what it is that you see or do not see."

"No." Although he was right, I did not like him to be critical of my mother.

"It's not the painting that is Catholic or Protestant," he said, "but the people who look at it, and what they expect to see. A painting in a church is like a candle in a dark room—we use it to see better. It is the bridge between ourselves and God. But it is not a Protestant candle or a Catholic candle. It is simply a candle."

"We do not need such things to help us to see God," I countered. "We have His Word, and that is enough."

He smiled. "Did you know, Griet, that I was brought up as a Protestant? I converted when I married. So you do not need to preach to me. I have heard such words before."

I stared at him. I had never known anyone to decide no longer to be a Protestant. I did not believe you really could switch. And yet he had.

He seemed to be waiting for me to speak.

"Though I have never been inside a Catholic church," I began slowly, "I think that if I

170

saw a painting there, it would be like yours. Even though they are not scenes from the Bible, or the Virgin and Child, or the Crucifixion." I shivered, thinking of the painting that had hung over my bed in the cellar.

He picked up the bottle again and carefully poured a few drops of oil into the shell. With his palette knife he began to mix the oil and white lead together until the paint was like butter that has been left out in a warm kitchen. I was bewitched by the movement of the silvery knife in the creamy white paint.

"There is a difference between Catholic and Protestant attitudes to painting," he explained as he worked, "but it is not necessarily as great as you may think. Paintings may serve a spiritual purpose for Catholics, but remember too that Protestants see God everywhere, in everything. By painting everyday things— tables and chairs, bowls and pitchers, soldiers and maids—are they not celebrating God's creation as well?"

I wished my mother could hear him. He would have made even her understand.

Catharina did not like to have her jewelry box left in the studio, where she could not get to it. She was suspicious of me, in part because she did not like me, but also because she was influenced by the stories we had all heard of maids stealing silver spoons from their mistresses. Stealing and tempting the master of the house—that was what mistresses were always looking for in maids.

As I had discovered with van Ruijven, however, it was more often the man pursuing the maid than the other way around. To him a maid came free.

Although she rarely consulted him about household things, Catharina went to her husband to ask that something be done. I did not hear them talk of it myself—Maertge told me one morning. Maertge and I got on well at that time. She had grown older suddenly, losing interest in the other children, preferring to be with me in the mornings as I went about my work. From me she learned to sprinkle clothes with water to bleach them in the sun, to apply a mixture of salt and wine to grease stains to get them out, to scrub the flatiron with coarse salt so that it would not stick and scorch. Her hands were too fine to work in water, however—she could watch me but I would not let her wet her hands. My own were ruined by now—hard and red and cracked, despite my mother's remedies to soften them. I had work hands and I was not yet eighteen.

Maertge was a little like my sister, Agnes, had been—lively, questioning, quick to decide what she thought. But she was also the eldest, with the eldest's seriousness of purpose. She had looked after her sisters, as I had looked after my brother and sister. That made a girl cautious and wary of change.

"Mama wants her jewelry box back," she announced as we passed around the star in

Market Square on our way to the Meat Hall. "She has spoken to Papa about it."

"What did she say?" I tried to sound unconcerned as I eyed the points of the star. I had noticed recently that when Catharina unlocked the studio door for me each morning she peered into the room at the table where her jewels lay.

Maertge hesitated. "Mama doesn't like it that you are locked up with her jewelry at night," she said at last. She did not add what Catharina was worried about—that I might pick up the pearls from the table, tuck the box under my arm, and climb from the window to the street, to escape to another city and another life.

In her way Maertge was trying to warn me. "She wants you to sleep downstairs again," she continued. "The nurse is leaving soon and there is no reason for you to remain in the attic. She said either you or the jewelry box must go."

"And what did your father say?"

"He didn't say anything. He will think about it."

My heart grew heavy like a stone in my chest. Catharina had asked him to choose between me and the jewelry box. He could not have both. But I knew he would not remove the box and pearls from the painting to keep me in the attic. He would remove me. I would no longer assist him.

I slowed my pace. Years of hauling water, wringing out clothes, scrubbing floors, emptying chamberpots, with no chance of beauty or color or light in my life, stretched before me like a landscape of flat land where, a long way off, the sea is visible but can never be reached. If I could not work with the colors, if I could not be near him, I did not know how I could continue to work in that house.

When we arrived at the butcher's stall and Pieter the son was not there, my eyes unexpectedly filled with tears. I had not realized that I had wanted to see his kind, handsome face. Confused as I felt about him, he was my escape, my reminder that there was another world I could join. Perhaps I was not so different from my parents, who looked on him to save them, to put meat on their table.

Pieter the father was delighted by my tears. "I will tell my son you wept to find him gone," he declared, scrubbing his chopping board clean of blood.

"You will do no such thing," I muttered. "Maertge, what do we want today?"

"Stewing beef," she answered promptly. "Four pounds."

I wiped my eyes with a corner of my apron. "There's a fly in my eye," I said briskly. "Perhaps it is not so clean around here. The dirt attracts flies."

Pieter the father laughed heartily. "Fly in her eye, she says! Dirt here. Of course there are flies—they come for the blood, not the dirt. The best meat is the bloodiest and attracts the most flies. You'll find out for yourself someday. No need to put on airs with us, madam." He winked at Maertge. "What do you think, miss? Should young Griet condemn a place when she'll be serving there herself in a few years?"

Maertge tried not to look shocked, but she was clearly surprised by his suggestion that I might not be with her family for always. She had the sense not to answer him—instead she took a sudden interest in the baby a woman at the next stall was holding.

"Please," I said in a low voice to Pieter the father, "don't say such things to her, or any of the family, even in jest. I am their maid. That is what I am. To suggest otherwise is to show them disrespect."

Pieter the father regarded me. His eyes changed color with every shift in the light. I did not think even my master could have captured them in paint. "Perhaps you're right," he conceded. "I can see I'll have to be more careful when I tease you. But I'll tell you one thing, my dear—you'd best get used to flies."

He did not remove the jewelry box, and he did not ask me to leave. Instead he brought the box and pearls and earrings to Catharina every evening, and she locked them away in the cupboard in the great hall where she kept the yellow mantle. In the morning when she unlocked the studio door to let me out she handed me the box and jewels. My first task in the studio became to place the box and pearls back on the table, and set out the earrings if van Ruijven's wife was coming to model. Catharina watched from the doorway as I made the measurements with my arms and hands. My gestures would have looked odd to anyone, but she never asked what I was doing. She did not dare.

Cornelia must have known about the problem with the jewelry box. Perhaps like Maertge she had overheard her parents discussing it. She may have seen Catharina bringing up the box in the morning and him carrying it down again at night, and guessed something was wrong. Whatever she saw or understood, she decided it was time to stir the pot once more.

For no particular reason but a vague distrust, she did not like me. She was very like her mother in that way.

She began it, as she had with the torn collar and the red paint on my apron, with a request. Catharina was dressing her hair one rainy morning, Cornelia idling at her side, watching. I was starching clothes in the washing kitchen so I did not hear them. But it was probably she who suggested that her mother wear tortoiseshell combs in her hair.

A few minutes later Catharina came to the doorway separating the washing and cooking kitchens and announced, "One of my combs is missing. Has either of you seen it?" Although she was speaking to both Tanneke and me, she was staring hard at me.

"No, madam," Tanneke replied solemnly, coming from the cooking kitchen to stand in the doorway as well so she could look at me.

"No, madam," I echoed. When I saw Cornelia peeking in from the hallway, with the mischievous look so natural to her, I knew she had begun something that would once again lead to me.

She will do this until she drives me away, I thought.

"Someone must know where it is," Catharina said.

"Shall I help you search the cupboard again, madam?" Tanneke asked. "Or shall we look elsewhere?" she added pointedly.

"Perhaps it is in your jewelry box," I suggested.

"Perhaps."

Catharina passed into the hallway. Cornelia turned and followed her.

I thought she would pay no attention to my suggestion, since it came from me. When I heard her on the stairs, however, I realized she was heading to the studio, and hurried to join her—she would need me. She was waiting, furious, in the studio doorway, Cornelia lingering behind her.

"Bring the box to me," Catharina ordered quietly, the humiliation of not being able to enter the room tingeing her words with an edge I had not heard before. She had often spoken sharply and loudly. The quiet control of her tone this time was much more frightening.

I could hear him in the attic. I knew what he was doing—he was grinding lapis for paint for the tablecloth.

I picked up the box and brought it to Catha-

177

rina, leaving the pearls on the table. Without a word she carried it downstairs, Cornelia once again trailing behind her like a cat thinking it is about to be fed. She would go to the great hall and sort through all her jewels, to see if anything else was missing. Perhaps other things were—it was hard to guess what a seven-year-old determined to make mischief might do.

She would not find the comb in her box. I knew exactly where it was.

I did not follow her, but climbed up to the attic.

He looked at me in surprise, his hand holding the muller suspended above the bowl, but he did not ask me why I had come upstairs. He began grinding again.

I opened the chest where I kept my things and unwrapped the comb from its handkerchief. I rarely looked at the comb—in that house I had no reason to wear it or even to admire it. It reminded me too much of the kind of life I could never have as a maid. Now that I knew to look at it closely, I could see it was not my grandmother's, though very similar. The scallop shape at the end of it was longer and more curved, and there were tiny serrated marks on each panel of the scallop. It was finer than my grandmother's, though not so much finer.

I wonder if I will ever see my grandmother's comb again, I thought.

I sat for so long on the bed, the comb in my lap, that he stopped grinding again.

"What is wrong, Griet?"

His tone was gentle. That made it easier to say what I had no choice but to say.

"Sir," I declared at last, "I need your help."

I remained in my attic room, sitting on my bed, hands in my lap, while he spoke to Catharina and Maria Thins, while they searched Cornelia, then searched among the girls' things for my grandmother's comb. Maertge finally found it, hidden in the large shell the baker had given them when he came to see his painting. That was probably when Cornelia had switched the combs, climbing down from the attic while the children were all playing in the storeroom and hiding my comb inside the first thing she could find.

It was Maria Thins who had to beat Cornelia—he made it clear it was not his duty, and Catharina refused to, even when she knew that Cornelia should be punished. Maertge told me later that Cornelia did not cry, but sneered throughout the beating.

It was Maria Thins too who came to see me in the attic. "Well, girl," she said, leaning against the grinding table, "you have set the cat loose in the poultry house now."

"I did nothing," I protested.

"No, but you have managed to make a few enemies. Why is that? We've never had so much trouble with other help." She chuckled, but behind her laugh she was sober. "But he has backed you, in his way," she continued, "and that is more powerful than anything Catharina or Cornelia or Tanneke or even I may say against you."

She tossed my grandmother's comb in my lap. I wrapped it in a handkerchief and replaced it in the chest. Then I turned to Maria Thins. If I did not ask her now, I would never know. This might be the only time she would be willing to answer me. "Please, madam, what did he say? About me?"

Maria Thins gave me a knowing look. "Don't flatter yourself, girl. He said very little about you. But it was clear enough. That he came downstairs at all and concerned himself—my daughter knew then that he was taking your side. No, he charged her with failing to raise her children properly. Much cleverer, you see, to criticize her than to praise you."

"Did he explain that I was—assisting him?"

"No."

I tried not to let my face show what I felt, but the very question must have made my feelings clear.

"But *I* told her, once he had gone," Maria Thins added. "It's nonsense, you sneaking around, keeping secrets from her in her own house." She sounded as if she were blaming me, but then she muttered, "I would have thought better of him." She stopped, looking as if she wished she hadn't revealed so much of her own mind.

"What did she say when you told her?"

"She's not happy, of course, but she's more afraid of his anger." Maria Thins hesitated. "There's another reason why she's not so concerned. I may as well tell you now. She's carrying a child again."

180

"Another?" I let slip. I was surprised that Catharina would want another child when they were so short of money.

Maria Thins frowned at me. "Watch yourself, girl."

"I'm sorry, madam." I instantly regretted having spoken even that one word. It was not for me to say how big their family should be. "Has the doctor been?" I asked, trying to make amends.

"Doesn't need to. She knows the signs, she's been through it enough." For a moment Maria Thins' face made clear her thoughts—she too wondered about so many children. Then she became stern again. "You go about your duties, stay out of her way, and help him, but don't parade it in front of the house. Your place here is not so secure."

I nodded and let my eyes rest on her gnarled hands as they fumbled with a pipe. She lit it and puffed for a moment. Then she chuckled. "Never so much trouble with a maid before. Lord love us!"

On Sunday I took the comb back to my mother. I did not tell her what had happened—I simply said it was too fine for a maid to keep.

Some things changed for me in the house after the trouble with the comb. Catharina's treatment of me was the greatest surprise. I had expected that she would be even more difficult than before—give me more work, berate me whenever she could, make me as uncomfortable as possible. Instead she seemed to fear me. She removed the studio key from the precious bunch at her hip and handed it back to Maria Thins, never locking or unlocking the door again. She left her jewelry box in the studio, sending her mother to fetch what she needed from it. She avoided me as much as she could. Once I understood this, I kept out of her way as well.

She did not say anything about my afternoon work in the attic. Maria Thins must have impressed upon her the notion that my help would make him paint more, and support the child she carried as well as those she had already. She had taken to heart his words about her care of the children, who were after all her main charge, and began to spend more time with them than she had before. With the encouragement of Maria Thins, she even began to teach Maertge and Lisbeth to read and write.

Maria Thins was more subtle, but she too changed toward me, treating me with more respect. I was still clearly a maid, but she did not dismiss me so readily, or ignore me, as she did sometimes with Tanneke. She would not go so far as to ask my opinion, but she made me feel less excluded from the household.

I was also surprised when Tanneke softened toward me. I had thought she enjoyed being angry and bearing me a grudge, but perhaps it had worn her out. Or perhaps once it was clear that he took my side, she felt it best not to appear to be opposed to me. Perhaps they all felt like that. Whatever the reason, she stopped creating extra work for me by spilling things, stopped muttering about me under her breath and giving me hard sideways looks. She did not befriend me, but it became easier to work with her.

It was cruel, perhaps, but I felt I had won a battle against her. She was older and had been a part of the household for much longer, but his favoring me clearly carried more weight than her loyalty and experience. She could have felt this slight deeply, but she accepted defeat more easily than I would have expected. Tanneke was a simple creature underneath, and wanted an easy time of it. The easiest way was to accept me.

Although her mother took closer charge of her, Cornelia did not change. She was Catharina's favorite, perhaps because she most resembled her in spirit, and Catharina would do little to tame her ways. Sometimes she looked at me with her light brown eyes, her head tilted so that her red curls dangled about her face, and I thought of the sneer Maertge had described as Cornelia's expression while she was being beaten. And I thought again, as I had on my first day: She will be a handful.

Though I did not make a show of it, I avoided Cornelia as I did her mother. I did not wish to encourage her. I hid the broken tile, my best lace collar, which my mother had made for me, and my finest embroidered handkerchief, so that she could not use them against me.

He did not treat me differently after the affair of the comb. When I thanked him for speaking up for me, he shook his head as if shooing away a fly that buzzed about him.

It was I who felt differently about him. I felt indebted. I felt that if he asked me to do something I could not say no. I did not know what he would ask that I would want to say no to, but nonetheless I did not like the position I had come to be in.

I was disappointed in him as well, though I did not like to think about it. I had wanted him to tell Catharina himself about my assisting him, to show that he was not afraid to tell her, that he supported me.

That is what I wanted.

Maria Thins came to see him in his studio one afternoon in the middle of October, when the painting of van Ruijven's wife was nearly complete. She must have known I was working in the attic and could hear her, but nevertheless she spoke directly to him.

She asked him what he intended to paint next. When he did not reply she said, "You must paint a larger painting, with more figures in it, as you used to. Not another woman alone with only her thoughts. When van Ruijven comes to see his painting you must suggest another

184

to him. Perhaps a companion piece to something you've already painted for him. He will agree—he usually does. And he will pay more for it."

He still did not respond.

"We're further in debt," Maria Thins said bluntly. "We need the money."

"He may ask that she be in it," he said. His voice was low but I was able to hear what he said, though only later did I understand what he meant.

"So?"

"No. Not like that."

"We'll worry about that when it happens, not before."

A few days later van Ruijven and his wife came to see the finished painting. In the morning my master and I prepared the room for their visit. He took the pearls and jewelry box down to Catharina while I put away everything else and set out chairs. Then he moved the easel and painting into the place where the setting had been and had me open all the shutters.

That morning I helped Tanneke prepare a special dinner for them. I did not think I would have to see them, and when they came at noon it was Tanneke who took up wine as they gathered in the studio. When she returned, however, she announced that I was to help her serve dinner rather than Maertge, who was old enough to join them at the table. "My mistress has decided this," she added.

I was surprised—the last time they viewed

their painting Maria Thins had tried to keep me away from van Ruijven. I did not say so to Tanneke, though. "Is van Leeuwenhoek there too?" I asked instead. "I thought I heard his voice in the hallway."

Tanneke nodded absently. She was tasting the roasted pheasant. "Not bad," she murmured. "I can hold my head as high as any cook of van Ruijven's."

While she was upstairs I had basted the pheasant and sprinkled it with salt, which Tanneke used too sparingly.

When they came down to dinner and everyone was seated, Tanneke and I began to bring in the dishes. Catharina glared at me. Never good at concealing her thoughts, she was horrified to see that I was serving.

My master too looked as if he had cracked his tooth on a stone. He stared coldly at Maria Thins, who feigned indifference behind her glass of wine.

Van Ruijven, however, grinned. "Ah, the wide-eyed maid!" he cried. "I wondered where you'd got to. How are you, my girl?"

"Very well, sir, thank you," I murmured, placing a slice of pheasant on his plate and moving away as quickly as I could. Not quickly enough, however—he managed to slide his hand along my thigh. I could still feel the ghost of it a few minutes later.

While van Ruijven's wife and Maertge remained oblivious, van Leeuwenhoek noted everything—Catharina's fury, my master's irritation, Maria Thins' shrug, van Ruijven's lingering hand. When I served him he searched my face as if looking there for the answer to how a simple maid could cause so much trouble. I was grateful to him—there was no blame in his expression.

Tanneke too had noticed the stir I caused, and for once was helpful. We said nothing in the kitchen, but it was she who made the trips back to the table to bring out the gravy, to refill the wine, to serve more food, while I looked after things in the kitchen. I had to go back only once, when we were both to clear away the plates. Tanneke went directly to van Ruijven's place while I took up plates at the other end of the table. Van Ruijven's eyes followed me everywhere.

So did my master's.

I tried to ignore them, instead listening to Maria Thins. She was discussing the next painting. "You were pleased with the one of the music lesson, weren't you?" she said. "What better to follow such a painting with than another with a musical setting? After a lesson, a concert, perhaps with more people in it, three or four musicians, an audience—"

"No audience," my master interrupted. "I do not paint audiences."

Maria Thins regarded him skeptically.

"Come, come," van Leeuwenhoek interjected genially, "surely an audience is less interesting than the musicians themselves."

I was glad he defended my master.

"I don't care about audiences," van Ruijven announced, "but I would like to be in the painting. I will play the lute." After a pause he added, "I want her in it too." I did not have to look at him to know he had gestured at me.

Tanneke jerked her head slightly towards the kitchen and I escaped with the little I had cleared, leaving her to gather the rest. I wanted to look at my master but did not dare. As I was leaving I heard Catharina say in a gay voice, "What a fine idea! Like that painting with you and the maid in the red dress. Do you remember her?"

On Sunday my mother spoke to me when we were alone in her kitchen. My father was sitting out in the late October sun while we prepared dinner. "You know I don't listen to market gossip," she began, "but it is hard not to hear it when my daughter's name is mentioned."

I immediately thought of Pieter the son. Nothing we did in the alley was worthy of gossip. I had insisted on that. "I don't know what you mean, Mother," I answered honestly.

My mother pulled in the corners of her mouth. "They are saying your master is going to paint you." It was as if the words themselves made her mouth purse.

I stopped stirring the pot I had been tending. "Who says this?"

My mother sighed, reluctant to pass along overheard tales. "Some women selling apples."

When I did not respond she took my silence

to mean the worst. "Why didn't you tell me, Griet?"

"Mother, I haven't even heard this myself. No one has said anything to me!"

She did not believe me.

"It's true," I insisted. "My master has said nothing, Maria Thins has said nothing. I simply clean his studio. That's as close as I get to his paintings." I had never told her about my attic work. "How can you believe old women selling apples rather than me?"

"When there's talk about someone at the market, there's usually a reason for it, even if it's not what's actually being said." My mother left the kitchen to call my father. She would say no more about the subject that day, but I began to fear she might be right—I would be the last to be told.

The next day at the Meat Hall I decided to ask Pieter the father about the rumor. I did not dare speak of it to Pieter the son. If my mother had heard the gossip, he would have as well. I knew he would not be pleased. Although he had never said so to me, it was clear he was jealous of my master.

Pieter the son was not at the stall. I did not have to wait long for Pieter the father to say something himself. "What's this I hear?" he smirked as I approached. "Going to have your picture painted, are you? Soon you'll be too grand for the likes of my son. He's gone off in a sulk to the Beast Market because of you."

"Tell me what you have heard."

"Oh, you want it told again, do you?" He raised his voice. "Shall I make it into a fine tale for a few others?"

"Hush," I hissed. Underneath his bravado I sensed he was angry with me. "Just tell me what you have heard."

Pieter the father lowered his voice. "Only that van Ruijven's cook was saying you are to sit with her master for a painting."

"I know nothing of this," I stated firmly, aware even as I said it that, as with my mother, my words had little effect. Pieter the father scooped up a handful of pigs' kidneys. "It's not me you should be talking to," he said, weighing them in his hand.

I waited a few days before speaking to Maria Thins. I wanted to see if anyone would tell me first. I found her in the Crucifixion room one afternoon when Catharina was asleep and Maertge had taken the girls to the Beast Market. Tanneke was in the kitchen sewing and watching Johannes and Franciscus.

"May I speak to you, madam?" I said in a low voice.

"What is it, girl?" She lit her pipe and regarded me through the smoke. "Trouble again?" She sounded weary.

"I don't know, madam. But I have heard a strange thing."

"So have we all heard strange things."

"I have heard that—that I am to be in a painting. With van Ruijven."

Maria Thins chuckled. "Yes, that is a strange

190

thing. They've been talking in the market, have they?"

I nodded.

She leaned back in her chair and puffed on her pipe. "Tell me, what would you think of being in such a painting?"

I did not know what to answer. "What would I think, madam?" I repeated dumbly.

"I wouldn't bother to ask some people that. Tanneke, for instance. When he painted her she stood there happily pouring milk for months without a thought passing through that head, God love her. But you—no, there's all manner of things you think but don't say. I wonder what they are?"

I said the one sensible thing I knew she would understand. "I do not wish to sit with van Ruijven, madam. I do not think his intentions are honorable." My words were stiff.

"His intentions are never honorable when it comes to young women."

I nervously wiped my hands on my apron.

"It seems you have a champion to defend your honor," she continued. "My son-in-law is no more willing to paint you with van Ruijven than you are willing to sit with him."

I did not try to hide my relief.

"But," Maria Thins warned, "van Ruijven is his patron, and a wealthy and powerful man. We cannot afford to offend him."

"What will you say to him, madam?"

"I'm still trying to decide. In the meantime, you will have to put up with the rumors.

Don't answer them—we don't want van Ruijven hearing from the market gossips that you are refusing to sit with him."

I must have looked uncomfortable. "Don't worry, girl," Maria Thins growled, tapping her pipe on the table to loosen the ash. "We'll take care of this. You keep your head down and go about your work, and not a word to anyone."

"Yes, madam."

I did tell one person, though. I felt I had to.

It had been easy enough to avoid Pieter the son—there were auctions all that week at the Beast Market, of animals that had been fattening all summer and autumn in the countryside and were ready for slaughter just before winter began. Pieter had gone every day to the sales.

The afternoon after Maria Thins and I spoke I slipped out to look for him at the market, just around the corner from the Oude Langendijck. It was quieter there in the afternoon than in the morning, when the auctions took place. By now many of the beasts had been driven away by their new owners, and men stood about under the plane trees that lined the square, counting their money and discussing the deals that had been made. The leaves on the trees had turned yellow and fallen to mingle with the dung and urine I could smell long before I reached the market.

Pieter the son was sitting with another man outside one of the taverns on the square, a tankard of beer in front of him. Deep in conversation, he did not see me as I stood silently near his table. It was his companion who looked up, then nudged Pieter.

"I would like to speak to you for a moment," I said quickly, before Pieter had a chance even to look surprised.

His companion immediately jumped up and offered me his chair.

"Could we walk?" I gestured to the square.

"Of course," Pieter said. He nodded to his friend and followed me across the street. From his expression it was not clear whether or not he was pleased to see me.

"How were the auctions today?" I asked awkwardly. I was never good at making everyday talk.

Pieter shrugged. He took my elbow to steer me around a pile of dung, then dropped his hand.

I gave up. "There has been gossip about me in the market," I said bluntly.

"There is gossip about everyone at one time or another," he replied neutrally.

"It's not true what they say. I'm not going to be in a painting with van Ruijven."

"Van Ruijven likes you. My father told me."

"But I'm not going to be in a painting with him."

"He is very powerful."

"You must believe me, Pieter."

"He is very powerful," he repeated, "and you are but a maid. Who do you think will win that round of cards?"

"You think I will become like the maid in the red dress."

"Only if you drink his wine." Pieter gazed at me levelly.

"My master does not want to paint me with van Ruijven," I said reluctantly after a moment. I had not wanted to mention him.

"That's good. I don't want him to paint you either."

I stopped and closed my eyes. The close animal smell was beginning to make me feel faint.

"You're getting caught where you should not be, Griet," Pieter said more kindly. "Theirs is not your world."

I opened my eyes and took a step back from him. "I came here to explain that the rumor is false, not to be accused by you. Now I'm sorry I bothered."

"Don't be. I do believe you." He sighed. "But you have little power over what happens to you. Surely you can see that?"

When I did not answer he added, "If your master did want to paint a picture of you and van Ruijven, do you really think you could say no?"

It was a question I had asked myself but found no answer to. "Thank you for reminding me of how helpless I am," I replied tartly.

"You wouldn't be, with me. We would run our own business, earn our own money, rule our own lives. Isn't that what you want?"

I looked at him, at his bright blue eyes, his yellow curls, his eager face. I was a fool even to hesitate.

"I didn't come here to talk about this. I'm

too young yet." I used the old excuse. Someday I would be too old to use it.

"I never know what you're thinking, Griet," he tried again. "You're so calm and quiet, you never say. But there are things inside you. I see them sometimes, hiding in your eyes."

I smoothed my cap, checking with my fingers for stray hairs. "All I mean to say is that there is no painting," I declared, ignoring what he had just said. "Maria Thins has promised me. But you're not to tell anyone. If they speak to you of me in the market, say nothing. Don't try to defend me. Otherwise van Ruijven may hear and your words will work against us."

Pieter nodded unhappily and kicked at a bit of dirty straw.

He will not always be so reasonable, I thought. One day he will give up.

To reward him for his reasonableness, I let him take me into a space between two houses off the Beast Market and run his hands down my body, cupping them where there were curves. I tried to take pleasure in it, but I was still feeling sick from the animal smell.

Whatever I said to Pieter the son, I myself did not feel reassured by Maria Thins' promise to keep me out of the painting. She was a formidable woman, astute in business, certain of her place, but she was not van Ruijven. I did not see how they could refuse him what he wanted. He had wanted a painting of his wife looking directly at the painter, and my master had made it. He had wanted a painting of the maid in the red dress, and had got that. If he wanted me, why should he not get me?

One day three men I had not seen before came with a harpsichord tied securely in a cart. A boy followed them carrying a bass viol that was bigger than he. They were not van Ruijven's instruments, but from one of his relations who was fond of music. The whole house gathered to watch the men struggle with the harpsichord on the steep stairs. Cornelia stood right at the bottom—if they were to drop the instrument it would fall directly on her. I wanted to reach out and pull her back, and if it had been one of the other children I would not have hesitated. Instead I remained where I was. It was Catharina who finally insisted that she move to a safer spot.

When they got it up the stairs they took it to the studio, my master supervising them. After the men left, he called down to Catharina. Maria Thins followed her up. A moment later we heard the sound of the harpsichord being played. The girls sat on the stairs while Tanneke and I stood in the hallway, listening.

"Is that the mistress playing? Or your mistress?" I asked Tanneke. It seemed so unlike either of them that I thought perhaps he was playing and simply wanted Catharina to be his audience.

"It's the young mistress, of course," Tanneke hissed. "Why would he have asked her up otherwise? She's very good, is the young mistress. She played when she was a girl. But her father kept their harpsichord when he and my mistress separated. Have you never heard young mistress complain about not being able to afford an instrument?"

"No." I thought for a moment. "Do you think he will paint her? For this painting with van Ruijven?" Tanneke must have heard the market gossip but had said nothing of it to me.

"Oh, the master never paints her. She can't sit still!"

Over the next few days he moved a table and chairs into the setting, and lifted the harpsichord's lid, which was painted with a landscape of rocks and trees and sky. He spread a table rug on the table in the foreground, and set the bass viol under it.

One day Maria Thins called me to the Crucifixion room. "Now, girl," she said, "this afternoon I want you to go on some errands for me. To the apothecary's for some elder flowers and hyssop—Franciscus has a cough now that it's cold again. And then to Old Mary the spinner for some wool, just enough for a collar for Aleydis. Did you notice hers is unravelling?" She paused, as if calculating how long it would take me to get from place to place. "And then go to Jan Mayer's house to ask when his brother is expected in Delft. He lives by the Rietveld Tower. That's near your parents, isn't it? You may stop in and visit them."

Maria Thins had never allowed me to see my parents apart from Sundays. Then I guessed. "Is van Ruijven coming today, madam?"

"Don't let him see you," she answered grimly. "It's best if you're not here at all. Then if he asks for you we can say you're out."

For a moment I wanted to laugh. Van Ruijven had us all—even Maria Thins—running like rabbits before dogs.

My mother was surprised to see me that afternoon. Luckily a neighbor was visiting and she could not question me closely. My father was not so interested. He had changed much since I'd left home, since Agnes had died. He was no longer so curious about the world outside his street, rarely asking me about the goings-on at the Oude Langendijck or in the market. Only the paintings still interested him.

"Mother," I announced as we sat by the fire, "my master is beginning the painting that you were asking about. Van Ruijven has come over and he is setting it up today. Everyone who is to be in the painting is there now."

Our neighbor, a bright-eyed old woman who loved market talk, gazed at me as if I had just set a roast capon in front of her. My mother frowned—she knew what I was doing.

There, I thought. That will take care of the rumors.

He was not himself that evening. I heard him snap at Maria Thins at supper, and he went out later and came back smelling of the tavern. I was climbing the stairs to bed when he came in. He looked up at me, his face tired and red. His expression was not angry, but weary, as of a man who has just seen all the wood he must chop, or a maid faced with a mountain of laundry.

The next morning the studio gave few clues about what had happened the afternoon before. Two chairs had been placed, one at the harpsichord, the other with its back to the painter. There was a lute on the chair, and a violin on the table to the left. The bass viol still lay in the shadows under the table. It was hard to tell from the arrangement how many people were to be in the painting.

Later Maertge told me that van Ruijven had come with his sister and one of his daughters.

"How old is the daughter?" I could not help asking.

"Seventeen, I think."

My age.

They came around again a few days later. Maria Thins sent me on more errands and told me to amuse myself elsewhere for the morning. I wanted to remind her that I could not stay away every day they came to be painted—it was getting too cold to idle in the streets, and there was too much work to do. But I did not say anything. I could not explain it, but I felt something was to change soon. I just did not know how.

I could not go to my parents again—they would think something was wrong, and explaining otherwise would make them believe even worse things were happening. Instead I went to Frans' factory. I had not seen him since he had asked me about the valuables in the house. His questions had angered me and I had made no effort to visit him.

The woman at the gate did not recognize me. When I asked to see Frans she shrugged and stepped aside, disappearing without showing me where to go. I walked into a low building where boys Frans' age sat on benches at long tables, painting tiles. They were working on simple designs, with nothing of the graceful style of my father's tiles. Many were not even painting the main figures, but only the flourishes in the corners of the tiles, the leaves and curlicues, leaving a blank center for a more skilled master to fill.

When they saw me a chorus of high whistles erupted that made me want to stop my ears. I went up to the nearest boy and asked him where my brother was. He turned red and ducked his head. Though I was a welcome distraction, no one would answer my question.

I found another building, smaller and hotter, housing the kiln. Frans was there alone, with his shirt off and the sweat pouring from him and a grim look on his face. The muscles in his arms and chest had grown. He was becoming a man.

He had tied quilted material around his forearms and hands that made him look clumsy, but when he pulled trays of tiles in and out of the kiln, he skillfully wielded the flat sheets so that he did not burn himself. I was afraid to call to him because he would be startled and might drop a tray. But he saw me before I spoke, and immediately set down the tray he held.

"Griet, what are you doing here? Is something wrong with Mother or Father?"

"No, no, they're fine. I've just come to visit."

"Oh." Frans pulled the cloths from his arms, wiped his face with a rag and gulped beer from a mug. He leaned against the wall and rolled his shoulders the way men do who have finished unloading cargo from a canal boat and are easing and stretching their muscles. I had never seen him make such a gesture before.

"Are you still working the kiln? They have not moved you to something else? Glazing, or painting like those boys in the other building?"

Frans shrugged.

"But those boys are the same age as you. Shouldn't you be—" I could not finish my sentence when I saw the look on his face.

"It's punishment," he said in a low voice.

"Why? Punishment for what?"

Frans did not answer.

"Frans, you must tell me or I'll tell our parents you're in trouble."

"I'm not in trouble," he said quickly. "I made the owner angry, is all."

"How?"

"I did something his wife didn't like."

"What did you do?"

Frans hesitated. "It was she who started it," he said softly. "She showed her interest, you see. But when I showed mine she told her husband. He didn't throw me out because he's a friend of Father's. So I'm on the kiln until his humor improves."

"Frans! How could you be so stupid? You know she's not for the likes of you. To endanger your place here for something like that?"

"You don't understand what it's like," Frans muttered. "Working here, it's exhausting, it's boring. It was something to think about, that's all. *You* have no right to judge, you with your butcher that you'll marry and have a fine life with. Easy for you to say what my life should be like when all I can see are endless tiles and long days. Why shouldn't I admire a pretty face when I see one?"

I wanted to protest, to tell him that I understood. At night I sometimes dreamed of piles of laundry that never got smaller no matter how much I scrubbed and boiled and ironed.

"Was she the woman at the gate?" I asked instead.

Frans shrugged and drank more beer. I pictured her sour expression and wondered how such a face could ever tempt him.

202

"Why are you here, anyway?" he asked. "Shouldn't you be at Papists' Corner?"

I had prepared an excuse for why I had come, that an errand had taken me to that part of Delft. But I felt so sorry for my brother that I found myself telling him about van Ruijven and the painting. It was a relief to confide in him.

He listened carefully. When I finished he declared, "You see, we're not so different, with the attentions we've had from those above us."

"But I haven't responded to van Ruijven, and have no intention to."

"I didn't mean van Ruijven," Frans said, his look suddenly sly. "No, not him. I meant your master."

"What about my master?" I cried.

Frans smiled. "Now, Griet, don't work yourself into a state."

"Stop that! What are you suggesting? He has never—"

"He doesn't have to. It's clear from your face. You want him. You can hide it from our parents and your butcher man, but you can't hide it from me. I know you better than that."

He did. He did know me better.

I opened my mouth but no words came out.

Although it was December, and cold, I walked so fast and fretted so much over Frans that I got back to Papists' Corner long before I should have. I grew hot and began to loosen my shawls to cool my face. As I was walking up the Oude Langendijck I saw van Ruijven and my master coming toward me. I bowed my head and crossed over so that I would pass by my master's side rather than van Ruijven's but the crossing only drew van Ruijven's attention to me. He stopped, forcing my master to halt with him.

"You—the wide-eyed maid," he called, turning towards me. "They told me you were out. I think you've been avoiding me. What's your name, my girl?"

"Griet, sir." I kept my eyes fixed on my master's shoes. They were shiny and black—Maertge had polished them under my guidance earlier that day.

"Well, Griet, have you been avoiding me?"

"Oh no, sir. I've been on errands." I held up a pail of things I had been to get for Maria Thins before I visited Frans.

"I hope I will see more of you, then."

"Yes, sir." Two women were standing behind the men. I peeked at their faces and guessed they were the daughter and sister who were sitting for the painting. The daughter was staring at me.

"You have not forgotten your promise, I hope," van Ruijven said to my master.

My master jerked his head like a puppet. "No," he replied after a moment.

"Good, I expect you'll want to make a start on that before you ask us to come again." Van Ruijven's smile made me shiver.

There was a long silence. I glanced at my master. He was struggling to maintain a calm expression, but I knew he was angry.

"Yes," he said at last, his eyes on the house opposite. He did not look at me.

I did not understand that conversation in the street, but I knew it was to do with me. The next day I discovered how.

In the morning he asked me to come up in the afternoon. I assumed he wanted me to work with the colors, that he was starting the concert painting. When I got to the studio he was not there. I went straight to the attic. The grinding table was clear—nothing had been laid out for me. I climbed back down the ladder, feeling foolish.

He had come in and was standing in the studio, looking out a window.

"Take a seat, please, Griet," he said, his back to me.

I sat in the chair by the harpsichord. I did not touch it—I had never touched an instrument except to clean it. As I waited I studied the paintings he had hung on the back wall that would form part of the concert painting. There was a landscape on the left, and on the right a picture of three people—a woman playing a lute, wearing a dress that revealed much of her bosom, a gentleman with his arm around her, and an old woman. The man was buying the young woman's favors, the old woman reaching to take the coin he held out. Maria Thins owned the painting and had told me it was called *The Procuress*.

"Not that chair." He had turned from the window. "That is where van Ruijven's daughter sits."

Where I would have sat, I thought, if I were to be in the painting.

He got another of the lion-head chairs and set it close to his easel but sideways so it faced the window. "Sit here."

"What do you want, sir?" I asked, sitting. I was puzzled—we never sat together. I shivered, although I was not cold.

"Don't talk." He opened a shutter so that the light fell directly on my face. "Look out the window." He sat down in his chair by the easel.

I gazed at the New Church tower and swallowed. I could feel my jaw tightening and my eyes widening.

"Now look at me."

I turned my head and looked at him over my left shoulder.

His eyes locked with mine. I could think of nothing except how their grey was like the inside of an oyster shell.

He seemed to be waiting for something. My face began to strain with the fear that I was not giving him what he wanted.

"Griet," he said softly. It was all he had to say. My eyes filled with tears I did not shed. I knew now.

"Yes. Don't move."

He was going to paint me.

1666

"You smell of linseed oil."

My father spoke in a baffled tone. He did not believe that simply cleaning a painter's studio would make the smell linger on my clothes, my skin, my hair. He was right. It was as if he guessed that I now slept with the oil in my room, that I sat for hours being painted and absorbing the scent. He guessed and yet he could not say. His blindness took away his confidence so that he did not trust the thoughts in his mind.

A year before I might have tried to help him, suggest what he was thinking, humor him into speaking his mind. Now, however, I simply watched him struggle silently, like a beetle that has fallen onto its back and cannot turn itself over.

My mother had also guessed, though she did not know what she had guessed. Sometimes I could not meet her eye. When I did her look was a puzzle of anger held back, of curiosity, of hurt. She was trying to understand what had happened to her daughter.

I had grown used to the smell of linseed oil. I even kept a small bottle of it by my bed. In the mornings when I was getting dressed I held it up to the window to admire the color, which was like lemon juice with a drop of lead-tin yellow in it.

I wear that color now, I wanted to say. He is painting me in that color.

Instead, to take my father's mind off the smell, I described the other painting my master was working on. "A young woman sits at a harpsichord, playing. She is wearing a yellow and black bodice—the same the baker's daughter wore for her painting—a white satin skirt and white ribbons in her hair. Standing in the curve of the harpsichord is another woman, who is holding music and singing. She wears a green, fur-trimmed housecoat and a blue dress. In between the women is a man sitting with his back to us—"

"Van Ruijven," my father interrupted.

"Yes, van Ruijven. All that can be seen of him is his back, his hair, and one hand on the neck of a lute."

"He plays the lute badly," my father added eagerly.

"Very badly. That's why his back is to us—so we won't see that he can't even hold his lute properly."

My father chuckled, his good mood restored. He was always pleased to hear that a rich man could be a poor musician.

It was not always so easy to bring him back into good humor. Sundays had become so

210

uncomfortable with my parents that I began to welcome those times when Pieter the son ate with us. He must have noted the troubled looks my mother gave me, my father's querulous comments, the awkward silences so unexpected between parent and child. He never said anything about them, never winced or stared or became tongue-tied himself. Instead he gently teased my father, flattered my mother, smiled at me.

Pieter did not ask why I smelled of linseed oil. He did not seem to worry about what I might be hiding. He had decided to trust me.

He was a good man.

I could not help it, though—I always looked to see if there was blood under his finger-nails.

He should soak them in salted water, I thought. One day I will tell him so.

He was a good man, but he was becoming impatient. He did not say so, but sometimes on Sundays in the alley off the Rietveld Canal, I could feel the impatience in his hands. He would grip my thighs harder than he needed, press his palm into my back so that I was glued in his groin and would know its bulge, even under many layers of cloth. It was so cold that we did not touch each other's skin—only the bumps and textures of wool, the rough outlines of our limbs.

Pieter's touch did not always repel me. Sometimes, if I looked over his shoulder at the sky, and found the colors besides white in a cloud, or thought of grinding lead white or mas-sicot, my breasts and belly tingled, and I pressed against him. He was always pleased when I responded. He did not notice that I avoided looking at his face and hands.

That Sunday of the linseed oil, when my father and mother looked so puzzled and unhappy, Pieter led me to the alley later. There he began squeezing my breasts and pulling at their nipples through the cloth of my dress. Then he stopped suddenly, gave me a sly look, and ran his hands over my shoulders and up my neck. Before I could stop him his hands were up under my cap and tangled in my hair.

I held my cap down with both hands. "No!"

Pieter smiled at me, his eyes glazed as if he had looked too long at the sun. He had managed to pull loose a strand of my hair, and tugged it now with his fingers. "Some day soon, Griet, I will see all of this. You will not always be a secret to me." He let a hand drop to the lower curve of my belly and pushed against me. "You will be eighteen next month. I'll speak to your father then."

I stepped back from him—I felt as if I were in a hot, dark room and could not breathe. "I am still so young. Too young for that."

Pieter shrugged. "Not everyone waits until they're older. And your family needs me." It was the first time he had referred to my parents' poverty, and their dependence on him— their dependence which became my dependence as well. Because of it they were content to take the gifts of meat and have me stand in an alley with him on a Sunday.

I frowned. I did not like being reminded of his power over us.

Pieter sensed that he should not have said anything. To make amends he tucked the strand of hair back under my cap, then touched my cheek. "I'll make you happy, Griet," he said. "I will."

After he left I walked along the canal, despite the cold. The ice had been broken so that boats could get through, but a thin layer had formed again on the surface. When we were children Frans and Agnes and I would throw stones to shatter the thin ice until every sliver had disappeared under water. It seemed a long time ago.

A month before he had asked me to come up to the studio.

"I will be in the attic," I announced to the room that afternoon.

Tanneke did not look up from her sewing. "Put some more wood on the fire before you go," she ordered.

The girls were working on their lace, overseen by Maertge and Maria Thins. Lisbeth had patience and nimble fingers, and produced good work, but Aleydis was still too young to manage the delicate weaving, and Cornelia too impatient. The cat sat at Cornelia's feet by the fire, and occasionally the girl reached down and dangled a bit of thread for the creature to paw at. Eventually, she probably hoped, the cat would tear its claws through her work and ruin it.

After feeding the fire I stepped around Johannes, who was playing with a top on the cold kitchen tiles. As I left he spun it wildly, and it hopped straight into the fire. He began to cry while Cornelia shrieked with laughter and Maertge tried to haul the toy from the flames with a pair of tongs.

"Hush, you'll wake Catharina and Franciscus," Maria Thins warned the children. They did not hear her.

I crept out, relieved to escape the noise, no matter how cold it would be in the studio.

The studio door was shut. As I approached it I pressed my lips together, smoothed my eyebrows, and ran my fingers down the sides of my cheeks to my chin, as if I were testing an apple to see if it was firm. I hesitated in front of the heavy wooden door, then knocked softly. There was no answer, though I knew he must be there—he was expecting me.

It was the first day of the new year. He had painted the ground layer of my painting almost a month before, but nothing since—no reddish marks to indicate the shapes, no false colors, no overlaid colors, no highlights. The canvas was a blank yellowish white. I saw it every morning as I cleaned.

I knocked louder.

When the door opened he was frowning, his eyes not catching mine. "Don't knock, Griet, just come in quietly," he said, turning away and going back to the easel, where the blank canvas sat waiting for its colors.

I closed the door softly behind me, blotting out the noise of the children downstairs, and stepped to the middle of the room. Now that the moment had come at last I was surprisingly calm. "You wanted me, sir."

"Yes. Stand over there." He gestured to the corner where he had painted the other women. The table he was using for the concert painting was set there, but he had cleared away the musical instruments. He handed me a letter. "Read that," he said.

I unfolded the sheet of paper and bowed my head over it, worried that he would discover I was only pretending to read an unfamiliar hand.

Nothing was written on the paper.

I looked up to tell him so, but stopped. With him it was often better to say nothing. I bowed my head again over the letter.

"Try this instead," he suggested, handing me a book. It was bound in worn leather and the spine was broken in several places. I opened it at random and studied a page. I did not recognize any of the words.

He had me sit with the book, then stand holding it while looking at him. He took away the book, handed me the white jug with the pewter top and had me pretend to pour a glass of wine. He asked me to stand and simply look out the window. All the while he seemed perplexed, as if someone had told him a story and he couldn't recall the ending.

"It is the clothes," he murmured. "That is the problem."

I understood. He was having me do things a lady would do, but I was wearing a maid's clothes. I thought of the yellow mantle and the yellow and black bodice, and wondered which he would ask me to wear. Instead of being excited by the idea, though, I felt uneasy. It was not just that it would be impossible to hide from Catharina that I was wearing her clothes. I did not feel right holding books and letters, pouring myself wine, doing things I never did. As much as I wanted to feel the soft fur of the mantle around my neck, it was not what I normally wore.

"Sir," I spoke finally, "perhaps you should have me do other things. Things that a maid does."

"What does a maid do?" he asked softly, folding his arms and raising his eyebrows.

I had to wait a moment before I could answer—my jaw was trembling. I thought of Pieter and me in the alley and swallowed. "Sewing," I replied. "Mopping and sweeping. Carrying water. Washing sheets. Cutting bread. Polishing windowpanes."

"You would like me to paint you with your mop?"

"It's not for me to say, sir. It is not my painting."

He frowned. "No, it is not yours." He sounded as if he were speaking to himself.

"I do not want you to paint me with my mop." I said it without knowing that I would.

"No. No, you're right, Griet. I would not paint you with a mop in your hand."

"But I cannot wear your wife's clothes."

There was a long silence. "No, I expect not," he said. "But I will not paint you as a maid."

"What, then, sir?"

"I will paint you as I first saw you, Griet. Just you."

He set a chair near his easel, facing the middle window, and I sat down. I knew it was to be my place. He was going to find the pose he had put me in a month before, when he had decided to paint me.

"Look out the window," he said.

I looked out at the grey winter day and, remembering when I stood in for the baker's daughter, tried not to see anything but to let my thoughts become quiet. It was hard because I was thinking of him, and of me sitting in front of him.

The New Church bell struck twice.

"Now turn your head very slowly towards me. No, not your shoulders. Keep your body turned towards the window. Move only your head. Slow, slow. Stop. A little more, so that—stop. Now sit still."

I sat still.

At first I could not meet his eyes. When I did it was like sitting close to a fire that suddenly blazes up. Instead I studied his firm chin, his thin lips.

"Griet, you are not looking at me."

I forced my gaze up to his eyes. Again I felt

as if I were burning, but I endured it—he wanted me to.

Soon it became easier to keep my eyes on his. He looked at me as if he were not seeing me, but someone else, or something else—as if he were looking at a painting.

He is looking at the light that falls on my face, I thought, not at my face itself. That is the difference.

It was almost as if I were not there. Once I felt this I was able to relax a little. As he was not seeing me, I did not see him. My mind began to wander—over the jugged hare we had eaten for dinner, the lace collar Lisbeth had given me, a story Pieter the son had told me the day before. After that I thought of nothing. Twice he got up to change the position of one of the shutters. He went to his cupboard several times to choose different brushes and colors. I viewed his movements as if I were standing in the street, looking in through the window.

The church bell struck three times. I blinked. I had not felt so much time pass. It was as if I had fallen under a spell.

I looked at him—his eyes were with me now. He was looking at me. As we gazed at each other a ripple of heat passed through my body. I kept my eyes on his, though, until at last he looked away and cleared his throat.

"That will be all, Griet. There is some bone for you to grind upstairs."

I nodded and slipped from the room, my heart pounding. He was painting me.

"Pull your cap back from your face," he said one day.

"Back from my face, sir?" I repeated dumbly, and regretted it. He preferred me not to speak, but to do as he said. If I did speak, I should say something worth the words.

He did not answer. I pulled the side of my cap that was closest to him back from my cheek. The starched tip grazed my neck.

"More," he said. "I want to see the line of your cheek."

I hesitated, then pulled it back further. His eyes moved down my cheek.

"Show me your ear."

I did not want to. I had no choice.

I felt under the cap to make sure no hair was loose, tucking a few strands behind my ear. Then I pulled it back to reveal the lower part of my ear.

The look on his face was like a sigh, though he did not make a sound. I caught a noise in my own throat and pushed it down so that it would not escape.

"Your cap," he said. "Take it off."

"No, sir."

"No?"

"Please do not ask me to, sir." I let the cloth of the cap drop so that my ear and cheek were covered again. I looked at the floor, the grey and white tiles extending away from me, clean and straight.

"You do not want to bare your head?"

"No."

"Yet you do not want to be painted as a maid, with your mop and your cap, nor as a lady, with satin and fur and dressed hair."

I did not answer. I could not show him my hair. I was not the sort of girl who left her head bare.

He shifted in his chair, then got up. I heard him go into the storeroom. When he returned, his arms were full of cloth, which he dropped in my lap.

"Well, Griet, see what you can do with this. Find something here to wrap your head in, so that you are neither a lady nor a maid." I could not tell if he was angry or amused. He left the room, shutting the door behind him.

I sorted through the cloth. There were three caps, all too fine for me, and too small to cover my head fully. There were pieces of cloth, left over from dresses and jackets Catharina had made, in yellows and browns, blues and greys.

I did not know what to do. I looked around as if I would find an answer in the studio. My eyes fell on the painting of *The Procuress*—the young woman's head was bare, her hair held back with ribbons, but the old woman wore a piece of cloth wrapped around her head, criss-crossing in and out of itself. Perhaps that is what he wants, I thought. Perhaps that is what women who are neither ladies nor maids nor the other do with their hair.

I chose a piece of brown cloth and took it into the storeroom, where there was a mirror.

I removed my cap and wound the cloth around my head as best I could, checking the painting to try to imitate the old woman's. I looked very peculiar.

I *should* let him paint me with a mop, I thought. Pride has made me vain.

When he returned and saw what I had done, he laughed. I had not heard him laugh often—sometimes with the children, once with van Leeuwenhoek. I frowned. I did not like being laughed at.

"I have only done what you asked, sir," I muttered.

He stopped chuckling. "You're right, Griet. I'm sorry. And your face, now that I can see more of it, it is—" He stopped, never finishing his sentence. I always wondered what he would have said.

He turned to the pile of cloth I had left on my chair. "Why did you choose brown," he asked, "when there are other colors?"

I did not want to speak of maids and ladies again. I did not want to remind him that blues and yellows were ladies' colors. "Brown is the color I usually wear," I said simply.

He seemed to guess what I was thinking. "Tanneke wore blue and yellow when I painted her some years ago," he countered.

"I am not Tanneke, sir."

"No, that you certainly are not." He pulled out a long, narrow band of blue cloth. "Nonetheless, I want you to try this."

I studied it. "That is not enough cloth to cover my head."

"Use this as well, then." He picked up a piece of yellow cloth that had a border of the same blue and held it out to me.

Reluctantly I took the two pieces of cloth back to the storeroom and tried again in front of the mirror. I tied the blue cloth over my forehead, with the yellow piece wound round and round, covering the crown of my head. I tucked the end into a fold at the side of my head, adjusted folds here and there, smoothed the blue cloth round my head, and stepped back into the studio.

He was looking at a book and did not notice as I slipped into my chair. I arranged myself as I had been sitting before. As I turned my head to look over my left shoulder, he glanced up. At the same time the end of the yellow cloth came loose and fell over my shoulder.

"Oh," I breathed, afraid that the cloth would fall from my head and reveal all my hair. But it held—only the end of the yellow cloth dangled free. My hair remained hidden.

"Yes," he said then. "That is it, Griet. Yes."

He would not let me see the painting. He set it on a second easel, angled away from the door, and told me not to look at it. I promised not to, but some nights I lay in bed and thought about wrapping my blanket around me and stealing downstairs to see it. He would never know.

But he would guess. I did not think I could sit with him looking at me day after day without guessing that I had looked at the painting. I could not hide things from him. I did not want to.

I was reluctant, too, to discover how it was that he saw me. It was better to leave that a mystery.

The colors he asked me to mix gave no clues as to what he was doing. Black, ocher, lead white, lead-tin yellow, ultramarine, red lake—they were all colors I had worked with before, and they could as easily have been used for the concert painting.

It was unusual for him to work on two paintings at once. Although he did not like switching back and forth between the two, it did make it easier to hide from others that he was painting me. A few people knew. Van Ruijven knew—I was sure it was at his request that my master was making the painting. My master must have agreed to paint me alone so that he would not have to paint me with van Ruijven. Van Ruijven would own the painting of me.

I was not pleased by this thought. Nor, I believed, was my master.

Maria Thins knew about the painting as well. It was she who probably made the arrangement with van Ruijven. And besides, she could still go in and out of the studio as she liked, and could look at the painting, as I was not allowed to. Sometimes she looked at me sideways with a curious expression she could not hide.

I suspected Cornelia knew about the painting. I caught her one day where she should not be, on the stairs leading to the studio. She would not say why she was there when I asked her, and I let her go rather than bring her to Maria Thins or Catharina. I did not dare stir things up, not while he was painting me.

Van Leeuwenhoek knew about the painting. One day he brought his camera obscura and set it up so they could look at me. He did not seem surprised to see me sitting in my chair—my master must have warned him. He did glance at my unusual head cloth, but did not comment.

They took turns using the camera. I had learned to sit without moving or thinking, and without being distracted by his gaze. It was harder, though, with the black box pointed at me. With no eyes, no face, no body turned towards me, only a box and a black robe covering a humped back, I became uneasy. I could no longer be sure of how they were looking at me.

I could not deny, however, that it was exciting to be studied so intently by two gentlemen, even if I could not see their faces.

My master left the room to find a soft cloth to polish the lens. Van Leeuwenhoek waited until his tread could be heard on the stairs, then said softly, "You watch out for yourself, my dear."

"What do you mean, sir?"

"You must know that he's painting you to satisfy van Ruijven. Van Ruijven's interest in you has made your master protective of you."

I nodded, secretly pleased to hear what I had suspected.

"Do not get caught in their battle. You could be hurt."

I was still holding the position I had assumed for the painting. Now my shoulders twitched of their own accord, as if I were shaking off a shawl. "I do not think he would ever hurt me, sir."

"Tell me, my dear, how much do you know of men?"

I blushed deeply and turned my head away. I was thinking of being in the alley with Pieter the son.

"You see, competition makes men possessive. He is interested in you in part because van Ruijven is."

I did not answer.

"He is an exceptional man," van Leeuwenhoek continued. "His eyes are worth a room full of gold. But sometimes he sees the world only as he wants it to be, not as it is. He does not understand the consequences for others of his point of view. He thinks only of himself and his work, not of you. You must take care then—" He stopped. My master's footsteps were on the stairs.

"Take care to do what, sir?" I whispered.

"Take care to remain yourself."

I lifted my chin to him. "To remain a maid, sir?"

"That is not what I mean. The women in his paintings—he traps them in his world. You can get lost there."

My master came into the room. "Griet, you have moved," he said.

"I am sorry, sir." I took up my position once more.

Catharina was six months pregnant when he began the painting of me. She was large already, and moved slowly, leaning against walls, grabbing the back of chairs, sinking heavily into one with a sigh. I was surprised by how hard she made carrying a child seem, given that she had done so several times already. Although she did not complain aloud, once she was big she made every movement seem like a punishment she was being forced to bear. I had not noticed this when she was carrying Franciscus, when I was new to the house and could barely see beyond the pile of laundry waiting for me each morning.

As she grew heavier Catharina became more and more absorbed in herself. She still looked after the children, with Maertge's help. She still concerned herself with the housekeeping, and gave Tanneke and me orders. She still shopped for the house with Maria Thins. But part of her was elsewhere, with the baby inside. Her harsh manner was rare now, and less deliberate. She slowed down, and though she was clumsy she broke fewer things.

I worried about her discovering the painting of me. Luckily the stairs to the studio were becoming awkward for her to climb, so that she was unlikely to fling open the studio door and discover me in my chair, him at his easel. And because it was winter she preferred to sit by the fire with the children and Tanneke and Maria Thins, or doze under a mound of blankets and furs.

The real danger was that she would find out from van Ruijven. Of the people who knew of the painting, he was the worst at keeping a secret. He came to the house regularly to sit for the concert painting. Maria Thins no longer sent me on errands or told me to make myself scarce when he came. It would have been impractical—there were only so many errands I could run. And she must have thought he would be satisfied with the promise of a painting, and would leave me alone.

He did not. Sometimes he sought me out, while I was washing or ironing clothes in the washing kitchen, or working with Tanneke in the cooking kitchen. It was not so bad when others were around—when Maertge was with me, or Tanneke, or even Aleydis, he simply called out, "Hello, my girl," in his honeyed voice and left me in peace. If I was alone, however, as I often was in the courtyard, hanging up laundry so it could catch a few minutes of pale winter sunlight, he would step into the enclosed space, and behind a sheet I had just hung, or one of my master's shirts, he would touch me. I pushed him away as politely as a maid can a gentleman. Nonetheless he managed to become familiar with the shape of my breasts and thighs under my clothes. He said things to me that I tried to forget, words I would never repeat to anyone else.

Van Ruijven always visited Catharina for a few minutes after sitting in the studio, his daughter and sister waiting patiently for him to finish gossiping and flirting. Although Maria Thins had told him not to say anything to Catharina about the painting, he was not a man to keep secrets quietly. He was very pleased that he was to have the painting of me, and he sometimes dropped hints about it to Catharina.

One day as I was mopping the hallway I overheard him say to her, "Who would you have your husband paint, if he could paint anyone in the world?"

"Oh, I don't think about such things," she laughed in reply. "He paints what he paints."

"I don't know about that." Van Ruijven worked so hard to sound sly that even Catharina could not miss the hint.

"What do you mean?" she demanded.

"Nothing, nothing. But you should ask him for a painting. He might not say no. He could paint one of the children—Maertge, perhaps. Or your own lovely self."

Catharina was silent. From the way van Ruijven quickly changed the subject he must have realized he had said something that upset her.

Another time when she asked if he enjoyed sitting for the painting he replied, "Not as much as I would if I had a pretty girl to sit with me.

But soon enough I'll have her anyway, and that will have to do, for now."

Catharina let this remark pass, as she would not have done a few months before. But then, perhaps it did not sound so suspicious to her since she knew nothing of the painting. I was horrified, though, and repeated his words to Maria Thins.

"Have you been listening behind doors, girl?" the old woman asked.

"I—" I could not deny it.

Maria Thins smiled sourly. "It's about time I caught you doing things maids are meant to do. Next you'll be stealing silver spoons."

I flinched. It was a harsh thing to say, especially after all the trouble with Cornelia and the combs. I had no choice, though—I owed Maria Thins a great deal. She must be allowed her cruel words.

"But you're right, van Ruijven's mouth is looser than a whore's purse," she continued. "I will speak to him again."

Saying something to him, however, was of little use—it seemed to spur him on even more to make suggestions to Catharina. Maria Thins took to being in the room with her daughter when he visited so that she could try to rein in his tongue.

I did not know what Catharina would do when she discovered the painting of me. And she would, one day—if not in the house, then at van Ruijven's, where she would be dining and look up and see me staring at her from a wall.

He did not work on the painting of me every day. He had the concert to paint as well, with or without van Ruijven and his women. He painted around them when they were not there, or asked me to take the place of one of the women—the girl sitting at the harpsichord, the woman standing next to it singing from a sheet of paper. I did not wear their clothes. He simply wanted a body there. Sometimes the two women came without van Ruijven, and that was when he worked best. Van Ruijven himself was a difficult model. I could hear him when I was working in the attic. He could not sit still, and wanted to talk and play his lute. My master was patient with him, as he would be with a child, but sometimes I could hear a tone creep into his voice and knew that he would go out that night to the tavern, returning with eyes like glittering spoons.

I sat for him for the other painting three or four times a week, for an hour or two each time. It was the part of the week I liked best, with his eyes on only me for those hours. I did not mind that it was not an easy pose to hold, that looking sideways for long periods of time gave me headaches. I did not mind when sometimes he had me move my head again and again so that the yellow cloth swung around, so that he could paint me looking as if I had just turned to face him. I did whatever he asked of me.

He was not happy, though. February passed and March arrived, with its days of ice and sun, and he was not happy. He had been working on the painting for almost two months, and though I had not seen it, I thought it must be close to done. He was no longer having me mix quantities of color for it, but used tiny amounts and made few movements with his brushes as I sat. I had thought I understood how he wanted me to be, but now I was not sure. Sometimes he simply sat and looked at me as if he were waiting for me to do something. Then he was not like a painter, but like a man, and it was hard to look at him.

One day he announced suddenly, as I was sitting in my chair, "This will satisfy van Ruijven, but not me."

I did not know what to say. I could not help him if I had not seen the painting. "May I look at the painting, sir?"

He gazed at me curiously.

"Perhaps I can help," I added, then wished I had not. I was afraid I had become too bold.

"All right," he said after a moment.

I got up and stood behind him. He did not turn round, but sat very still. I could hear him breathing slowly and steadily.

The painting was like none of his others. It was just of me, of my head and shoulders, with no tables or curtains, no windows or powder-brushes to soften and distract. He had painted me with my eyes wide, the light falling across my face but the left side of me in shadow. I was wearing blue and yellow and brown. The cloth wound round my head made me look not like myself, but like Griet from another town, even from another country altogether. The background was black, making me appear very much alone, although I was clearly looking at someone. I seemed to be waiting for something I did not think would ever happen.

He was right—the painting might satisfy van Ruijven, but something was missing from it.

I knew before he did. When I saw what was needed—that point of brightness he had used to catch the eye in other paintings—I shivered. This will be the end, I thought.

I was right.

This time I did not try to help him as I had with the painting of van Ruijven's wife writing a letter. I did not creep into the studio and change things—reposition the chair I sat in or open the shutters wider. I did not wrap the blue and yellow cloth differently or hide the top of my chemise. I did not bite my lips to make them redder, or suck in my cheeks. I did not set out colors I thought he might use.

I simply sat for him, and ground and washed the colors he asked for.

He would find it for himself anyway.

It took longer than I had expected. I sat for him twice more before he discovered what was missing. Each time I sat he painted with a dissatisfied look on his face, and dismissed me early.

232

I waited.

Catharina herself gave him the answer. One afternoon Maertge and I were polishing shoes in the washing kitchen while the other girls had gathered in the great hall to watch their mother dress for a birth feast. I heard Aleydis and Lisbeth squeal, and knew Catharina had brought out her pearls, which the girls loved.

Then I heard his tread in the hallway, silence, then low voices. After a moment he called out, "Griet, bring my wife a glass of wine."

I set the white jug and two glasses on a tray, in case he chose to join her, and took them to the great hall. As I entered I bumped against Cornelia, who had been standing in the doorway. I managed to catch the jug, and the glasses clattered against my chest without breaking. Cornelia smirked and stepped out of my way.

Catharina was sitting at the table with her powder-brush and jar, her combs and jewelry box. She was wearing her pearls and her green silk dress, altered to cover her belly. I placed a glass near her and poured.

"Would you like some wine too, sir?" I asked, glancing up. He was leaning against the cupboard that surrounded the bed, pressed against the silk curtains, which I noticed for the first time were made of the same cloth as Catharina's dress. He looked back and forth between Catharina and me. On his face was his painter's look.

"Silly girl, you've spilled wine on me!" Catharina pushed away from the table and brushed at her belly with her hand. A few drops of red had splashed there.

"I'm sorry, madam. I'll get a damp cloth to sponge it."

"Oh, never mind. I can't bear to have you fussing about me. Just go."

I stole a look at him as I picked up the tray. His eyes were fixed on his wife's pearl earring. As she turned her head to brush more powder on her face the earring swung back and forth, caught in the light from the front windows. It made us all look at her face, and reflected light as her eyes did.

"I must go upstairs for a moment," he said to Catharina. "I won't be long."

That is it, then, I thought. He has his answer.

When he asked me to come to the studio the next afternoon, I did not feel excited as I usually did when I knew I was to sit for him. For the first time I dreaded it. That morning the clothes I washed felt particularly heavy and sodden, and my hands not strong enough to wring them well. I moved slowly between the kitchen and the courtyard, and sat down to rest more than once. Maria Thins caught me sitting when she came in for a copper pancake pan. "What's the matter, girl? Are you ill?" she asked.

I jumped up. "No, madam. Just a little tired."

"Tired, eh? That's no way for a maid to be,

234

especially not in the morning." She looked as if she did not believe me.

I plunged my hands into the cooling water and pulled out one of Catharina's chemises. "Are there any errands you would like me to run this afternoon, madam?"

"Errands? This afternoon? I don't think so. That's a funny thing to ask if you're feeling tired." She narrowed her eyes. "You aren't in trouble, are you, girl? Van Ruijven didn't catch you alone, did he?"

"No, madam." In fact he had, just two days before, but I had managed to pull away from him.

"Has someone discovered you upstairs?" Maria Thins asked in a low voice, jerking her head up to indicate the studio.

"No, madam." For a moment I was tempted to tell her about the earring. Instead I said, "I ate something that did not agree with me, that is all."

Maria Thins shrugged and turned away. She still did not believe me, but had decided it did not matter.

That afternoon I plodded up the stairs, and paused before the studio door. This would not be like other times when I sat for him. He was going to ask me for something, and I was beholden to him.

I pushed open the door. He sat at his easel, studying the tip of one of his brushes. When he looked up at me I saw something I had never before seen in his face. He was nervous.

That was what gave me the courage to say

what I said. I went to stand by my chair and placed my hand on one of the lion heads. "Sir," I began, gripping the hard, cool carving, "I cannot do it."

"Do what, Griet?" He was genuinely surprised.

"What you are going to ask me to do. I cannot wear it. Maids do not wear pearls."

He stared at me for a long moment, then shook his head a few times. "How unexpected you are. You always surprise me."

I ran my fingers around the lion's nose and mouth and up its muzzle to its mane, smooth and knobbled. His eyes followed my fingers.

"You know," he murmured, "that the painting needs it, the light that the pearl reflects. It won't be complete otherwise."

I did know. I had not looked at the painting long—it was too strange seeing myself—but I had known immediately that it needed the pearl earring. Without it there were only my eyes, my mouth, the band of my chemise, the dark space behind my ear, all separate. The earring would bring them together. It would complete the painting.

It would also put me on the street. I knew that he would not borrow an earring from van Ruijven or van Leeuwenhoek or anyone else. He had seen Catharina's pearl and that was what he would make me wear. He used what he wanted for his paintings, without considering the result. It was as van Leeuwenhoek had warned me.

When Catharina saw her earring in the painting she would explode.

I should have begged him not to ruin me.

"You are painting it for van Ruijven," I argued instead, "not for yourself. Does it matter so much? You said yourself that he would be satisfied with it."

His face hardened and I knew I had said the wrong thing.

"I would never stop working on a painting if I knew it was not complete, no matter who was to get it," he muttered. "That is not how I work."

"No, sir." I swallowed and gazed at the tiled floor. Stupid girl, I thought, my jaw tightening.

"Go and prepare yourself."

Bowing my head, I hurried to the storeroom where I kept the blue and yellow cloths. I had never felt his disapproval so strongly. I did not think I could bear it. I removed my cap and, feeling the ribbon that tied up my hair was coming undone, I pulled it off. I was reaching back to gather up my hair again when I heard one of the loose floor tiles in the studio clink. I froze. He had never come into the storeroom while I was changing. He had never asked that of me.

I turned round, my hands still in my hair. He stood on the threshold, gazing at me.

I lowered my hands. My hair fell in waves over my shoulders, brown like fields in the autumn. No one ever saw it but me.

"Your hair," he said. He was no longer angry.

At last he let me go with his eyes.

237

Now that he had seen my hair, now that he had seen me revealed, I no longer felt I had something precious to hide and keep to myself. I could be freer, if not with him, then with someone else. It no longer mattered what I did and did not do.

That evening I slipped from the house and found Pieter the son at one of the taverns where the butchers drank, near the Meat Hall. Ignoring the whistles and remarks, I went up to him and asked him to come with me. He set down his beer, his eyes wide, and followed me outside, where I took his hand and led him to a nearby alley. There I pulled up my skirt and let him do as he liked. Clasping my hands around his neck, I held on while he found his way into me and began to push rhythmically. He gave me pain, but when I remembered my hair loose around my shoulders in the studio, I felt something like pleasure too.

Afterwards, back at Papists' Corner, I washed myself with vinegar.

When I next looked at the painting he had added a wisp of hair peeking out from the blue cloth above my left eye.

The next time I sat for him he did not mention the earring. He did not hand it to me, as I had feared, or change how I sat, or stop painting.

He did not come into the storeroom again to see my hair either.

He sat for a long time, mixing colors on his palette with his palette knife. There was red and ocher there, but the paint he was mixing was mostly white, to which he added daubs of black, working them together slowly and carefully, the silver diamond of the knife flashing in the grey paint.

"Sir?" I began.

He looked up at me, his knife stilled.

"I have seen you paint sometimes without the model being here. Could you not paint the earring without me wearing it?"

The palette knife remained still. "You would like me to imagine you wearing the pearl, and paint what I imagine?"

"Yes, sir."

He looked down at the paint, the palette knife moving again. I think he smiled a little. "I want to see you wear the earring."

"But you know what will happen then, sir."

"I know the painting will be complete."

You will ruin me, I thought. Again I could not bring myself to say it. "What will your wife say when she sees the finished painting?" I asked instead, as boldly as I dared.

"She will not see it. I will give it directly to van Ruijven." It was the first time he had admitted he was painting me secretly, that Catharina would disapprove.

"You need only wear it once," he added, as if to placate me. "The next time I paint you

I will bring it. Next week. Catharina will not miss it for an afternoon."

"But, sir," I said, "my ear is not pierced."

He frowned slightly. "Well, then, you will need to take care of that." This was clearly a woman's detail, not something he felt he need concern himself with. He tapped the knife and wiped it with a rag. "Now, let us begin. Chin down a bit." He gazed at me. "Lick your lips, Griet."

I licked my lips.

"Leave your mouth open."

I was so surprised by this request that my mouth remained open of its own will. I blinked back tears. Virtuous women did not open their mouths in paintings.

It was as if he had been in the alley with Pieter and me.

You have ruined me, I thought. I licked my lips again.

"Good," he said.

I did not want to do it to myself. I was not afraid of pain, but I did not want to take a needle to my own ear.

If I could have chosen someone to do it for me, it would have been my mother. But she would never have understood, nor agreed to it without knowing why. And if she had been told why, she would have been horrified.

I could not ask Tanneke, or Maertge.

I considered asking Maria Thins. She may

240

not yet have known about the earring, but she would find out soon enough. I could not bring myself to ask her, though, to have her take part in my humiliation.

The only person who might do it and understand was Frans. I slipped out the next afternoon, carrying a needlecase Maria Thins had given me. The woman with the sour face at the factory gate smirked when I asked to see him.

"He's long gone and good riddance," she answered, relishing the words.

"Gone? Gone where?"

The woman shrugged. "Towards Rotterdam, they say. And then, who knows? Perhaps he'll make his fortune on the seas, if he doesn't die between the legs of some Rotterdam whore." These last bitter words made me look at her more closely. She was with child.

Cornelia had not known when she broke the tile of Frans and me that she would come to be right—that he would split from me and from the family. Will I ever see him again? I thought. And what will our parents say? I felt more alone than ever.

The next day I stopped at the apothecary's on my way back from the fish stalls. The apothecary knew me now, even greeting me by name. "And what is it that he wants today?" he asked. "Canvas? Vermilion? Ocher? Linseed oil?"

"He does not need anything," I answered nervously. "Nor my mistress. I have come—" For a moment I considered asking him to pierce my ear. He seemed a discreet man, who might do it without telling anyone or demanding to know why.

I could not ask a stranger such a thing. "I need something to numb the skin," I said.

"Numb the skin?"

"Yes. As ice does."

"Why do you want to numb the skin?"

I shrugged and did not answer, studying the bottles on the shelves behind him.

"Clove oil," he said at last with a sigh. He reached behind him for a flask. "Rub a little on the spot and leave it for a few minutes. It doesn't last long, though."

"I would like some, please."

"And who is to pay for this? Your master? It is very dear, you know. It comes from far away." In his voice was a mixture of disapproval and curiosity.

"I will pay. I only want a little." I removed a pouch from my apron and counted the precious stuivers onto the table. A tiny bottle of it cost me two days' wages. I had borrowed some money from Tanneke, promising to repay her when I was paid on Sunday.

When I handed over my reduced wages to my mother that Sunday I told her I had broken a hand mirror and had to pay for it.

"It will cost more than two days' wages to replace that," she scolded. "What were you doing, looking at yourself in a mirror? How careless."

"Yes," I agreed. "I have been very careless."

I waited until late, when I was sure everyone in the house was asleep. Although usually no one came up to the studio after it was locked for the night, I was still fearful of someone catching me, with my needle and mirror and clove oil. I stood by the locked studio door, listening. I could hear Catharina pacing up and down the hallway below. She was having a hard time sleeping now—her body had become too cumbersome to find a position she could lie in comfortably. Then I heard a child's voice, a girl's, trying to speak low but unable to hide its bright ring. Cornelia was with her mother. I could not hear what they said, and because I was locked into the studio, I could not creep to the top of the stairs to listen more closely.

Maria Thins was also moving about in her rooms next to the storeroom. It was a restless house, and it made me restless too. I made myself sit in my lion-head chair to wait. I was not sleepy. I had never felt so awake.

Finally Catharina and Cornelia went back to bed, and Maria Thins stopped rustling next door. As the house grew still, I remained in my chair. It was easier to sit there than do what I had to do. When I could not delay any longer, I got up and first peeked at the painting. All I could really see now was the great hole where the earring should go, which I would have to fill.

I took up my candle, found the mirror in the

storeroom, and climbed to the attic. I propped the mirror against the wall on the grinding table and set the candle next to it. I got out my needlecase and, choosing the thinnest needle, set the tip in the flame of the candle. Then I opened the bottle of clove oil, expecting it to smell foul, of mould or rotting leaves, as remedies often do. Instead it was sweet and strange, like honeycakes left out in the sun. It was from far away, from places Frans might get to on his ships. I shook a few drops onto a rag, and swabbed my left earlobe. The apothecary was right—when I touched the lobe a few minutes later it felt as if I had been out in the cold without wrapping a shawl around my ears.

I took the needle out of the flame and let the glowing red tip change to dull orange and then to black. When I leaned towards the mirror I gazed at myself for a moment. My eyes were full of liquid in the candlelight, glittering with fear.

Do this quickly, I thought. It will not help to delay.

I pulled the earlobe taut and in one movement pushed the needle through my flesh.

Just before I fainted I thought, I have always wanted to wear pearls.

Every night I swabbed my ear and pushed a slightly larger needle through the hole to keep it open. It did not hurt too much until the lobe became infected and began to swell. Then no matter how much clove oil I dabbed on the ear, my eyes streamed with tears when I drove the needle through. I did not know how I would manage to wear the earring without fainting again.

I was grateful that I wore my cap over my ears so that no one saw the swollen red lobe. It throbbed as I bent over the steaming laundry, as I ground colors, as I sat in church with Pieter and my parents.

It throbbed when van Ruijven caught me hanging up sheets in the courtyard one morning and tried to pull my chemise down over my shoulders and expose my bosom.

"You shouldn't fight me, my girl," he murmured as I backed away from him. "You'll enjoy it more if you don't fight. And you know, I will have you anyway when I get that painting." He pushed me against the wall and lowered his lips to my chest, pulling at my breasts to free them from the dress.

"Tanneke!" I called desperately, hoping in vain that she had returned early from an errand to the baker's.

"What are you doing?"

Cornelia was watching us from the doorway. I had never expected to be glad to see her.

Van Ruijven raised his head and stepped back. "We're playing a game, dear girl," he replied, smiling. "Just a little game. You'll play it too when you're older." He straightened his cloak and stepped past her into the house.

I could not meet Cornelia's eye. I tucked in

my chemise and smoothed my dress with shaking hands. When finally I looked up she was gone.

The morning of my eighteenth birthday I got up and cleaned the studio as usual. The concert painting was done—in a few days van Ruijven would come to view it and take it away. Although I did not need to now, I still cleaned the studio scene carefully, dusting the harpsichord, the violin, the bass viol, brushing the table rug with a damp cloth, polishing the chairs, mopping the grey and white floor tiles.

I did not like the painting as much as his others. Although it was meant to be more valuable with three figures in it, I preferred the pictures he had painted of women alone—they were purer, less complicated. I found I did not want to look at the concert for long, or try to understand what the people in it were thinking.

I wondered what he would paint next.

Downstairs I set water on the fire to heat and asked Tanneke what she wanted from the butcher. She was sweeping the steps and tiles in front of the house. "A rack of beef," she replied, leaning against her broom. "Why not have something nice?" She rubbed her lower back and groaned. "It may take my mind off my aches."

"Is it your back again?" I tried to sound sympathetic, but Tanneke's back always hurt. A maid's back would always hurt. That was a maid's life.

Maertge came with me to the Meat Hall, and I was glad of it—since that night in the alley I was embarrassed to be alone with Pieter the son. I was not sure how he would treat me. If I was with Maertge, however, he would have to be careful of what he said or did.

Pieter the son was not there—only his father, who grinned at me. "Ah, the birthday maid!" he cried. "An important day for you."

Maertge looked at me in surprise. I had not mentioned my birthday to the family—there was no reason to.

"There's nothing important about it," I snapped.

"That's not what my son said. He's off now, on an errand. Someone to see." Pieter the father winked at me. My blood chilled. He was saying something without saying it, something I was meant to understand.

"Your finest rack of beef," I ordered, deciding to ignore him.

"In celebration, then?" Pieter the father never let things drop, but pushed them as far as he could.

I did not reply. I simply waited until he served me, then put the beef in my pail and turned away.

"Is it really your birthday, Griet?" Maertge whispered as we left the Meat Hall.

"Yes."

"How old are you?"

"Eighteen."

"Why is eighteen so important?"

"It's not. You mustn't listen to what he says—he's a silly man."

Maertge didn't look convinced. Nor was I. His words had tugged at something in my mind.

I worked all morning rinsing and boiling laundry. My mind turned to many things while I sat over the tub of steaming water. I wondered where Frans was, and if my parents had heard yet that he had left Delft. I wondered what Pieter the father had meant earlier, and where Pieter the son was. I thought of the night in the alley. I thought of the painting of me, and wondered when it would be done and what would happen to me then. All the while my ear throbbed, stabbing with pain whenever I moved my head.

It was Maria Thins who came to get me.

"Leave your washing, girl," I heard her say behind me. "He wants you upstairs." She was standing in the doorway, shaking something in her hand.

I got up in confusion. "Now, madam?"

"Yes, now. Don't be coy with me, girl. You know why. Catharina has gone out this morning, and she doesn't do that much these days, now her time is closer. Hold out your hand."

I dried a hand on my apron and held it out. Maria Thins dropped a pair of pearl earrings into my palm.

"Take them up with you now. Quickly."

I could not move. I was holding two pearls

the size of hazelnuts, shaped like drops of water. They were silvery grey, even in the sunlight, except for a dot of fierce white light. I had touched pearls before, when I brought them upstairs for van Ruijven's wife and tied them round her neck or laid them on the table. But I had never held them for myself before.

"Go on, girl," Maria Thins growled impatiently. "Catharina may come back sooner than she said."

I stumbled into the hallway, leaving the laundry unwrung. I climbed the stairs in full view of Tanneke, who was bringing in water from the canal, and Aleydis and Cornelia, who were rolling marbles in the hallway. They all looked up at me.

"Where are you going?" Aleydis asked, her grey eyes bright with interest.

"To the attic," I replied softly.

"Can we come with you?" Cornelia said in a taunting voice.

"No."

"Girls, you're blocking my way." Tanneke pushed past them, her face dark.

The studio door was ajar. I stepped inside, pressing my lips together, my stomach twisting. I closed the door behind me.

He was waiting for me. I held my hand out to him and dropped the earrings into his palm.

He smiled at me. "Go and wrap up your hair."

I changed in the storeroom. He did not

come to look at my hair. As I returned I glanced at *The Procuress* on the wall. The man was smiling at the young woman as if he were squeezing pears in the market to see if they were ripe. I shivered.

He was holding up an earring by its wire. It caught the light from the window, capturing it in a tiny panel of bright white.

"Here you are, Griet." He held out the pearl to me.

"Griet! Griet! Someone is here to see you!" Maertge called from the bottom of the stairs.

I stepped to the window. He came to my side and we looked out.

Pieter the son was standing in the street below, arms crossed. He glanced up and saw us standing together at the window. "Come down, Griet," he called. "I want to speak to you." He looked as if he would never move from his spot.

I stepped back from the window. "I'm sorry, sir," I said in a low voice. "I won't be long." I hurried to the storeroom, pulled off the headcloths and changed into my cap. He was still standing at the window, his back to me, as I passed through the studio.

The girls were sitting in a row on the bench, staring openly at Pieter, who stared back at them.

"Let's go around the corner," I whispered, moving towards the Molenpoort. Pieter did not follow, but continued to stand with his arms crossed.

"What were you wearing up there?" he asked. "On your head."

I stopped and turned back. "My cap."

"No, it was blue and yellow."

Five sets of eyes watched us—the girls on the bench, him at the window. Then Tanneke appeared in the doorway, and that made six.

"Please, Pieter," I hissed. "Let's go along a little way."

"What I have to say can be said in front of anyone. I have nothing to hide." He tossed his head, his blond curls falling around his ears.

I could see he would not be silenced. He would say what I dreaded he would say in front of them all.

Pieter did not raise his voice, but we all heard his words. "I've spoken to your father this morning, and he has agreed that we may marry now you are eighteen. You can leave here and come to me. Today."

I felt my face go hot, whether from anger or shame I was not sure. Everyone was waiting for me to speak.

I drew in a deep breath. "This is not the place to talk about such things," I replied severely. "Not in the street like this. You were wrong to come here." I did not wait for his response, though as I turned to go back inside he looked stricken.

"Griet!" he cried.

I pushed past Tanneke, who spoke so softly that I was not sure I heard her right. "Whore."

I ran up the stairs to the studio. He was still

standing at the window as I shut the door. "I am sorry, sir," I said. "I'll just change my cap."

He did not turn round. "He is still there," he said.

When I returned, I crossed to the window, though I did not stand too close in case Pieter could see me again with my head wrapped in blue and yellow.

My master was not looking down at the street any longer, but at the New Church tower. I peeked—Pieter was gone.

I took my place in the lion-head chair and waited.

When he turned at last to face me, his eyes were masked. More than ever, I did not know what he was thinking.

"So you will leave us," he said.

"Oh, sir, I do not know. Do not pay attention to words said in the street like that."

"Will you marry him?"

"Please do not ask me about him."

"No, perhaps I should not. Now, let us begin again." He reached around to the cupboard behind him, picked up an earring, and held it out to me.

"I want you to do it." I had not thought I could ever be so bold.

Nor had he. He raised his eyebrows and opened his mouth to speak, but did not say anything.

He stepped up to my chair. My jaw tightened but I managed to hold my head steady. He reached over and gently touched my earlobe.

I gasped as if I had been holding my breath under water.

He rubbed the swollen lobe between his thumb and finger, then pulled it taut. With his other hand he inserted the earring wire in the hole and pushed it through. A pain like fire jolted through me and brought tears to my eyes.

He did not remove his hand. His fingers brushed against my neck and along my jaw. He traced the side of my face up to my cheek, then blotted the tears that spilled from my eyes with his thumb. He ran his thumb over my lower lip. I licked it and tasted salt.

I closed my eyes then and he removed his fingers. When I opened them again he had gone back to his easel and taken up his palette.

I sat in my chair and gazed at him over my shoulder. My ear was burning, the weight of the pearl pulling at the lobe. I could not think of anything but his fingers on my neck, his thumb on my lips.

He looked at me but did not begin to paint. I wondered what he was thinking.

Finally he reached behind him again. "You must wear the other one as well," he declared, picking up the second earring and holding it out to me.

For a moment I could not speak. I wanted him to think of me, not of the painting.

"Why?" I finally answered. "It can't be seen in the painting."

"You must wear both," he insisted. "It is a farce to wear only one."

"But—my other ear is not pierced," I faltered.

"Then you must tend to it." He continued to hold it out.

I reached over and took it. I did it for him. I got out my needle and clove oil and pierced my other ear. I did not cry, or faint, or make a sound. Then I sat all morning and he painted the earring he could see, and I felt, stinging like fire in my other ear, the pearl he could not see.

The clothes soaking in the kitchen went cold, the water grey. Tanneke clattered in the kitchen, the girls shouted outside, and we behind our closed door sat and looked at each other. And he painted.

When at last he set down his brush and palette, I did not change position, though my eyes ached from looking sideways. I did not want to move.

"It is done," he said, his voice muffled. He turned away and began wiping his palette knife with a rag. I gazed at the knife—it had white paint on it.

"Take off the earrings and give them back to Maria Thins when you go down," he added.

I began to cry silently. Without looking at him, I got up and went into the storeroom, where I removed the blue and yellow cloth from my head. I waited for a moment, my hair out over my shoulders, but he did not come. Now that the painting was finished he no longer wanted me.

I looked at myself in the little mirror, and

then I removed the earrings. Both holes in my lobes were bleeding. I blotted them with a bit of cloth, then tied up my hair and covered it and my ears with my cap, leaving the tips to dangle below my chin.

When I came out again he was gone. He had left the studio door open for me. For a moment I thought about looking at the painting to see what he had done, to see it finished, the earring in place. I decided to wait until night, when I could study it without worrying that someone might come in.

I crossed the studio and shut the door behind me.

I always regretted that decision. I never got to have a proper look at the finished painting.

Catharina arrived back only a few minutes after I had handed the earrings to Maria Thins, who immediately replaced them in the jewelry box. I hurried to the cooking kitchen to help Tanneke with dinner. She would not look at me straight, but gave me sideways glances, occasionally shaking her head.

He was not at dinner—he had gone out. After we had cleared up I went back to the court-yard to finish rinsing the laundry. I had to haul in new water and reheat it. While I worked Catharina slept in the great hall. Maria Thins smoked and wrote letters in the Crucifixion room. Tanneke sat in the front doorway and sewed. Maertge perched on the bench and made lace. Next to her Aleydis and Lisbeth sorted their shell collection.

I did not see Cornelia.

I was hanging up an apron when I heard Maria Thins say, "Where are you going?" It was the tone of her voice rather than what she said that made me pause in my work. She sounded anxious.

I crept inside and along the hallway. Maria Thins was at the foot of the stairs, gazing up. Tanneke had come to stand in the front doorway, as she had earlier that day, but facing in and following the look of her mistress. I heard the stairs creak, and the sound of heavy breathing. Catharina was pulling herself up the stairs.

In that moment I knew what was going to happen—to her, to him, to me.

Cornelia is there, I thought. She is leading her mother to the painting.

I could have cut short the misery of waiting. I could have left then, walked out the door with the laundry not done, and not looked back. But I could not move. I stood frozen, as Maria Thins stood frozen at the bottom of the stairs. She too knew what would happen, and she could not stop it.

I sank to the floor. Maria Thins saw me but did not speak. She continued to gaze up uncertainly. Then the noise on the stairs stopped and we heard Catharina's heavy tread over to the studio door. Maria Thins darted up the stairs. I remained on my knees, too weary to rise. Tanneke stood blocking the light from the front door. She watched me, her arms crossed, her face expressionless.

Soon after there was a shout of rage, then raised voices which were quickly lowered.

Cornelia came down the stairs. "Mama wants Papa to come home," she announced to Tanneke.

Tanneke stepped backwards outside and turned towards the bench. "Maertge, go and find your father at the Guild," she ordered. "Quickly. Tell him it's important."

Cornelia look around. When she saw me her face lit up. I got up from my knees and walked stiffly back to the courtyard. There was nothing I could do but hang up laundry and wait.

When he returned I thought for a moment that he might come and find me in the court-yard, hidden among the hanging sheets. He did not—I heard him on the stairs, then nothing.

I leaned against the warm brick wall and gazed up. It was a bright, cloudless day, the sky a mocking blue. It was the kind of day when children ran up and down the streets and shouted, when couples walked out through the town gates, past the windmills and along the canals, when old women sat in the sun and closed their eyes. My father was probably sitting on the bench in front of his house, his face turned towards the warmth. Tomorrow might be bitterly cold, but today it was spring.

They sent Cornelia to get me. When she

appeared between the hanging clothes and looked down at me with a cruel smirk on her face, I wanted to slap her as I had that first day I had come to work at the house. I did not, though—I simply sat, hands in my lap, shoulders slumped, and watched her show off her glee. The sun caught glints of gold—traces of her mother—in her red hair.

"You are wanted upstairs," she said in a formal voice. "They want to see you." She turned and skipped back into the house.

I leaned over and brushed a bit of dust from my shoe. Then I stood, straightened my skirt, smoothed my apron, pulled the tips of my cap tight, and checked for loose strands of hair. I licked my lips and pressed them together, took a deep breath and followed Cornelia.

Catharina had been crying—her nose was red, her eyes puffy. She was sitting in the chair he normally pulled up to his easel—it had been pushed towards the wall and the cupboard that held his brushes and palette knife. When I appeared she heaved herself up so that she was standing, tall and broad. Although she glared at me, she did not speak. She squeezed her arms over her belly and winced.

Maria Thins was standing next to the easel, looking sober but also impatient, as if she had other, more important things to attend to.

He stood next to his wife, his face without expression, hands at his sides, eyes on the painting. He was waiting for someone, for Catharina, or Maria Thins, or me, to begin.

I came to stand just inside the door. Cornelia hovered behind me. I could not see the painting from where I stood.

It was Maria Thins who finally spoke.

"Well, girl, my daughter wants to know how you came to be wearing her earrings." She said it as if she did not expect me to answer.

I studied her old face. She was not going to admit to helping me get the earrings. Nor would he, I knew. I did not know what to say. So I did not say anything.

"Did you steal the key to my jewelry box and take my earrings?" Catharina spoke as if she were trying to convince herself of what she said. Her voice was shaky.

"No, madam." Although I knew it would be easier for everyone if I said I had stolen them, I could not lie about myself.

"Don't lie to me. Maids steal all the time. You took my earrings!"

"Are they missing now, madam?"

For a moment Catharina looked confused, as much by my asking a question as by the question itself. She had obviously not checked her jewelry box since seeing the painting. She had no idea if the earrings were gone or not. But she did not like me asking the questions. "Quiet, thief. They'll throw you in prison," she hissed, "and you won't see sunlight for years." She winced again. Something was wrong with her.

"But, madam—"

"Catharina, you must not get yourself into a state," he interrupted me. "Van Ruijven will take the painting away as soon as it is dry and you can put it from your mind."

He did not want me to speak either. It seemed no one did. I wondered why they had asked me upstairs at all when they were so afraid of what I might say.

I might say, "What about the way he looked at me for so many hours while he painted this painting?" I might say, "What about your mother and your husband, who have gone behind your back and deceived you?"

Or I might simply say, "Your husband touched me, here, in this room."

They did not know what I might say.

Catharina was no fool. She knew the real matter was not the earrings. She wanted them to be, she tried to make them be so, but she could not help herself. She turned to her husband. "Why," she asked, "have you never painted me?"

As they gazed at each other it struck me that she was taller than he, and, in a way, more solid.

"You and the children are not a part of this world," he said. "You are not meant to be."

"And she is?" Catharina cried shrilly, jerking her head at me.

He did not answer. I wished that Maria Thins and Cornelia and I were in the kitchen or the Crucifixion room, or out in the market. It was an affair for a man and his wife to discuss alone.

"And with *my* earrings?"

Again he was silent, which stirred Catharina

even more than his words had. She began to shake her head so that her blond curls bounced around her ears. "I will not have this in my own house," she declared. "I will not have it!" She looked around wildly. When her eyes fell on the palette knife a shiver ran through me. I took a step forward at the same time as she moved to the cupboard and grabbed the knife. I stopped, unsure of what she would do next.

He knew, though. He knew his own wife. He moved with Catharina as she stepped up to the painting. She was quick but he was quicker—he caught her by the wrist as she plunged the diamond blade of the knife towards the painting. He stopped it just before the blade touched my eye. From where I stood I could see the wide eye, a flicker of earring he had just added, and the winking of the blade as it hovered before the painting. Catharina struggled but he held her wrist firmly, waiting for her to drop the knife. Suddenly she groaned. Flinging the knife away, she clutched her belly. The knife skidded across the tiles to my feet, then spun and spun, slower and slower, as we all stared at it. It came to a stop with the blade pointed at me.

I was meant to pick it up. That was what maids were meant to do—pick up their master's and mistress's things and put them back in their place.

I looked up and met his eye, holding his grey gaze for a long moment. I knew it was for the last time. I did not look at anyone else.

In his eyes I thought I could see regret.

I did not pick up the knife. I turned and walked from the room, down the stairs and through the doorway, pushing aside Tanneke. When I reached the street I did not look back at the children I knew must be sitting on the bench, nor at Tanneke, who would be frowning because I had pushed her, nor up at the windows, where he might be standing. I got to the street and I began to run. I ran down the Oude Langendijck and across the bridge into Market Square.

Only thieves and children run.

I reached the center of the square and stopped in the circle of tiles with the eight-pointed star in the middle. Each point indicated a direction I could take.

I could go back to my parents.

I could find Pieter at the Meat Hall and agree to marry him.

I could go to van Ruijven's house—he would take me in with a smile.

I could go to van Leeuwenhoek and ask him to take pity on me.

I could go to Rotterdam and search for Frans.

I could go off on my own somewhere far away.

I could go back to Papists' Corner.

. I could go into the New Church and pray to God for guidance.

I stood in the circle, turning round and round as I thought.

When I made my choice, the choice I knew I had to make, I set my feet carefully along the edge of the point and went the way it told me, walking steadily.

1676

When I looked up and saw her I almost dropped my knife. I had not set eyes on her in ten years. She looked almost the same, though she had grown a little broader, and as well as the old pockmarks, her face now carried scars up one side—Maertge, who still came to see me from time to time, had told me of the accident, the mutton joint that spat hot oil.

She had never been good at roasting meat.

She was standing far enough away that it was not clear she had indeed come to see me. I knew, though, that this could be no chance. For ten years she had managed to avoid me in what was not a big town. I had not once run into her in the market or the Meat Hall, or along any of the main canals. But then, I did not walk along the Oude Langendijck.

She approached the stall reluctantly. I set down my knife and wiped my bloody hands on my apron. "Hello, Tanneke," I said calmly, as if I had only seen her a few days before. "How have you been keeping?"

"Mistress wants to see you," Tanneke said bluntly, frowning. "You're to come to the house this afternoon."

It had been many years since someone had ordered me about in that tone. Customers asked for things, but that was different. I could refuse them if I didn't like what I heard.

"How is Maria Thins?" I asked, trying to remain polite. "And how is Catharina?"

"As well as can be expected, given what's happened."

"I expect they will manage."

"My mistress has had to sell some property, but she's being clever with the arrangements. The children will be all right." As in the past, Tanneke could not resist praising Maria Thins to anyone who would listen, even if it meant being too eager with details.

Two women had come up and were standing behind Tanneke, waiting to be served. Part of me wished they were not there so that I could ask her more questions, lead her to give away other details, to tell me much more about so many things. But another part of me—the sensible part that I had held to now for many years—did not want to have anything to do with her. I did not want to hear.

The women shifted from side to side as Tanneke stood solidly in front of the stall, still frowning but with a softer face. She pondered the cuts of meat laid out before her.

"Would you like to buy something?" I asked.

My question snapped her out of her stupor. "No," she muttered.

They bought their meat now from a stall at the far end of the Meat Hall. As soon as I began working alongside Pieter they had switched butchers—so abruptly that they did not even pay their bill. They still owed us fifteen guilders. Pieter never asked them for it. "It's the price I have paid for you," he sometimes teased. "Now I know what a maid is worth."

I did not laugh when he said this.

I felt a tiny hand tugging at my dress and looked down. Little Frans had found me and was clinging to my skirt. I touched the top of his head, full of blond curls like his father's. "There you are," I said. "Where's Jan and your grandmother?"

He was too young to be able to tell me, but I then saw my mother and elder son coming through the stalls towards me.

Tanneke looked back and forth between my sons and her face hardened. She darted a look at me full of blame, but she did not say what she was thinking. She stepped back, treading on the foot of the woman directly behind her. "Mind you come this afternoon," she said, then turned away before I could reply.

They had eleven children now—Maertge and market gossip had kept count for me. Yet Catharina had lost the baby she delivered that day of the painting and the palette knife. She gave birth in the studio itself—she could not get down the stairs to her own bed. The baby had come a month early and was small and sickly. It died not long after its birth

267

feast. I knew that Tanneke blamed me for the death.

Sometimes I pictured his studio with Catharina's blood on the floor and wondered how he was able still to work there.

Jan ran to his little brother and pulled him into a corner, where they began to kick a bone back and forth between them.

"Who was that?" my mother asked. She had never seen Tanneke.

"A customer," I replied. I often shielded her from things I knew would disturb her. Since my father's death she had become skittish as a wild dog about the new, the different, the changed.

"She didn't buy anything," my mother remarked.

"No. We didn't have what she wanted." I turned to wait on the next customer before my mother could ask more questions.

Pieter and his father appeared, carrying a side of beef between them. They flung it onto the table behind their stall and took up their knives. Jan and little Frans left their bone and ran over to watch. My mother stepped back—she had never grown used to the sight of so much meat. "I'll be getting along," she said, picking up her shopping pail.

"Can you watch the boys this afternoon? I have some errands to run."

"Where are you going?"

I raised my eyebrows. I had complained before to my mother that she asked too many questions. She had grown old and suspicious when there was usually nothing to be suspicious of. Now, though, when there was something to hide from her, I found myself strangely calm. I did not answer her question.

It was easier with Pieter. He simply glanced up at me from his work. I nodded at him. He had decided long ago not to ask questions, even though he knew I had thoughts sometimes that I did not speak of. When he removed my cap on our wedding night and saw the holes in my ears he did not ask.

The holes were long healed now. All that was left of them were tiny buds of hard flesh I could feel only if I pressed the lobes hard between my fingers.

It had been two months since I had heard the news. For two months now I could walk around Delft without wondering if I would see him. Over the years I had occasionally spotted him in the distance, on his way to or from the Guild, or near his mother's inn, or going to van Leeuwenhoek's house, which was not far from the Meat Hall. I never went near him, and I was not sure if he ever saw me. He strode along the streets or across the square with his eyes fixed on a distant point—not rudely or deliberately, but as if he were in a different world.

At first it was very hard for me. When I saw him I froze wherever I was, my chest tightened, and I could not get my breath. I had to hide my response from Pieter the father and son, from my mother, from the curious market gossips.

For a long time I thought I might still matter to him.

After a while, though, I admitted to myself that he had always cared more for the painting of me than for me.

It grew easier to accept this when Jan was born. My son made me turn inward to my family, as I had done when I was a child, before I became a maid. I was so busy with him that I did not have time to look out and around me. With a baby in my arms I stopped walking round the eight-pointed star in the square and wondering what was at the end of each of its points. When I saw my old master across the square my heart no longer squeezed itself like a fist. I no longer thought of pearls and fur, nor longed to see one of his paintings.

Sometimes on the streets I ran into the others—Catharina, the children, Maria Thins. Catharina and I turned our faces from each other. It was easier that way. Cornelia looked through me with disappointed eyes. I think she had hoped to destroy me completely. Lisbeth was kept busy looking after the boys, who were too young to remember me. And Aleydis was like her father—her grey eyes looked about her without settling on anything near to her. After a time there were other children I did not know, or knew only by their father's eyes or their mother's hair.

Of all of them, only Maria Thins and

Maertge acknowledged me, Maria Thins nodding briefly when she saw me, Maertge sneaking away to the Meat Hall to speak with me. It was Maertge who brought me my things from the house—the broken tile, my prayer book, my collars and caps. It was Maertge who told me over the years of his mother's death and of how he had to take over the running of her inn, of their growing debt, of Tanneke's accident with the oil.

It was Maertge who announced gleefully one day, "Papa has been painting me in the manner in which he painted you. Just me, looking over my shoulder. They are the only paintings he has done like that, you know."

Not exactly in the manner, I thought. Not exactly. I was surprised, though, that she knew of the painting. I wondered if she had seen it.

I had to be careful with her. For a long time she was but a girl, and I did not feel it right to ask too much about her family. I had to wait patiently for her to pass me tidbits of news. By the time she was old enough to be more frank with me, I was not so interested in her family now that I had my own.

Pieter tolerated her visits but I knew she made him uneasy. He was relieved when Maertge married a silk merchant's son and began to see less of me, and bought her meat from another butcher.

Now after ten years I was being called back to the house I had run from so abruptly.

Two months before, I had been slicing

tongue at the stall when I heard a woman waiting her turn say to another, "Yes, to think of dying and leaving eleven children and the widow in such debt."

I looked up and the knife cut deep into my palm. I did not feel the pain of it until I had asked, "Who are you speaking of?" and the woman replied, "The painter Vermeer is dead."

I scrubbed my fingernails especially hard when I finished at the stall. I had long ago given up always scrubbing them thoroughly, much to Pieter the father's amusement. "You see, you've grown used to stained fingers as you got used to the flies," he liked to say. "Now you know the world a little better you can see there's no reason always to keep your hands clean. They just get dirty again. Cleanliness is not as important as you thought back when you were a maid, eh?" Sometimes, though, I crushed lavender and hid it under my chemise to mask the smell of meat that seemed to hang about me even when I was far from the Meat Hall.

There were many things I'd had to get used to.

I changed into another dress, a clean apron, and a newly starched cap. I still wore my cap in the same way, and I probably looked much as I had the day I first set out to work as a maid. Only now my eyes were not so wide and innocent.

Although it was February, it was not bitterly cold. Many people were out in Market Square—our customers, our neighbors, people who knew us and would note my first step onto the Oude Langendijck in ten years. I would have to tell Pieter eventually that I had gone there. I did not know yet if I would need to lie to him about why.

I crossed the square, then the bridge leading from it over the canal to the Oude Langendijck. I did not hesitate, for I did not want to bring more attention to myself. I turned briskly and walked up the street. It was not far—in half a minute I was at the house—but it felt long to me, as if I were travelling to a strange city I had not visited for many years.

Because it was a mild day, the door was open and there were children sitting on the bench—four of them, two boys and two girls, lined up as their older sisters had been ten years before when I first arrived. The eldest was blowing bubbles, as Maertge had, though he laid down his pipe the moment he saw me. He looked to be ten or eleven years old. After a moment I realized he must be Franciscus, though I did not see much of the baby in him that I had known. But then, I had not thought much of babies when I was young. The others I did not recognize, except for seeing them occasionally in town with the older girls. They all stared at me.

I addressed myself to Franciscus. "Please tell your grandmother that Griet is here to see her."

Franciscus turned to the older of the two girls. "Beatrix, go and find Maria Thins."

The girl jumped up obediently and went inside. I thought of Maertge and Cornelia's scramble to announce me so long ago and smiled to myself.

The children continued to stare at me. "I know who you are," Franciscus declared.

/ "I doubt you can remember me, Franciscus. You were but a baby when I knew you."

He ignored my remark—he was following his own thought. "You're the lady in the painting."

I started, and Franciscus smiled in triumph. "Yes, you are, though in the painting you're not wearing a cap, but a fancy blue and yellow headcloth."

"Where is this painting?"

He seemed surprised that I should ask. "With van Ruijven's daughter, of course. He died last year, you know."

I had heard this news at the Meat Hall with secret relief. Van Ruijven had never sought me out once I'd left, but I had always feared that he would appear again one day with his oily smile and groping hands.

"How did you see the painting if it is at van Ruijven's?"

"Papa asked to have the painting on a short loan," Franciscus explained. "The day after Papa died Mama sent it back to van Ruijven's daughter."

I rearranged my mantle with shaking hands. "He wanted to see the painting again?" I managed to say in a small voice.

"Yes, girl." Maria Thins had come to stand in the doorway. "It didn't help matters here, I can tell you. But by that time he was in such a state that we didn't dare say no, not even Catharina." She looked exactly the same—she would never age. One day she would simply go to sleep and not wake up.

I nodded to her. "I'm sorry for your loss and your troubles, madam."

"Yes, well, life is a folly. If you live long enough, nothing is surprising."

I did not know how to respond to such words, so I simply said what I knew to be true. "You wanted to see me, madam."

"No, it's Catharina who is to see you."

"Catharina?" I could not keep the surprise from my voice.

Maria Thins smiled sourly. "You never did learn to keep your thoughts to yourself, did you, girl? Never mind, I expect you get by well enough with your butcher, if he doesn't ask too much of you."

I opened my mouth to speak, then shut it.

"That's right. You're learning. Now, Catharina and van Leeuwenhoek are in the great hall. He is the executor of the will, you see."

I did not see. I wanted to ask her what she meant, and why van Leeuwenhoek was there, but I did not dare. "Yes, madam," I said simply.

Maria Thins chuckled briefly. "The most trouble we've ever had with a maid," she muttered, shaking her head before disappearing inside.

I stepped into the front hallway. There were still paintings hanging everywhere on the walls, some I recognized, others I did not. I half expected to see myself among the still lifes and seascapes, but of course I was not there.

I glanced at the stairs leading up to his studio and stopped, my chest tightening. To stand in the house again, his room above me, was more than I thought I could bear, even though I knew he was not there. For so many years I had not let myself think of the hours I spent grinding colors at his side, sitting in the light of the windows, watching him look at me. For the first time in two months I became fully aware that he was dead. He was dead and he would paint no more paintings. There were so few—I had heard that he never did paint faster, as Maria Thins and Catharina had wanted him to.

It was only when a girl poked her head out from the Crucifixion room that I forced myself to take a deep breath and walk down the hallway towards her. Cornelia was now about the age I had been when I first became a maid. Her red hair had darkened over the ten years and was simply dressed, without ribbons or braids. She had grown less menacing to me over time. In fact I almost pitied her—her face was twisted by a cunning that gave a girl her age an ugly look.

I wondered what would happen to her, what would happen to them all. Despite Tanneke's confidence in her mistress's ability to arrange things, it was a big family, with a big debt. I had heard in the market that they had not paid their bill to the baker in three years, and after my master's death the baker had taken pity on Catharina and accepted a painting to settle the debt. For a brief moment I wondered if Catharina was going to give me a painting too, to settle her debt with Pieter.

Cornelia pulled her head back into the room and I stepped into the great hall. It had not changed much since I had worked there. The bed still had its green silk curtains, now faded. The ivory-inlaid cupboard was there, and the table and Spanish leather chairs, and the paintings of his family and hers. Everything appeared older, dustier, more battered. The red and brown floor tiles were cracked or missing in places.

Van Leeuwenhoek was standing with his back to the door, his hands clasped behind him, studying a painting of soldiers drinking in a tavern. He turned around and bowed to me, still the kind gentleman.

Catharina was seated at the table. She was not wearing black as I had expected. I did not know if she meant to taunt me, but she wore the yellow mantle trimmed with ermine. It too had a faded look about it, as if it had been worn too many times. There were badly repaired rents in the sleeves, and the fur had been eaten away in places by moths. Nonetheless, she was playing her part as the elegant lady of the house. She had dressed her hair carefully and was wearing powder and her pearl necklace.

She was not wearing the earrings.

Her face did not match her elegance. No amount of powder could mask her rigid anger, her reluctance, her fear. She did not want to meet with me, but she had to.

"Madam, you wished to see me." I thought it best to address myself to her, though I looked at van Leeuwenhoek as I spoke.

"Yes." Catharina did not gesture to a chair, as she would have to another lady. She let me stand.

There was an awkward silence as she sat and I stood, waiting for her to begin. She was clearly struggling to speak. Van Leeuwenhoek shifted from one foot to the other.

I did not try to help her. There seemed to be no way that I could. I watched her hands shuffle some papers on the table, run along the edges of the jewelry box at her elbow, pick up the powder-brush and set it down again. She wiped her hands on a white cloth.

"You know that my husband died two months ago?" she began at last.

"I had heard, madam, yes. I was very sorry to hear of it. May God keep him."

Catharina did not seem to take in my feeble words. Her mind was elsewhere. She picked up the brush again and ran her fingers through its bristles.

"It was the war with France, you see, that brought us to this state. Not even van Ruijven wanted to buy paintings then. And my mother had problems collecting her rents. And he had to take over the mortgage on his mother's inn. So it is no wonder things grew so difficult."

The last thing I had expected from Catharina was an explanation of why they ran into debt. Fifteen guilders after all this time is not so very much, I wanted to say. Pieter has let it go. Think no more of it. But I dared not interrupt her.

"And then there were the children. Do you know how much bread eleven children eat?" She looked up at me briefly, then back down at the powder-brush.

One painting's worth over three years, I answered silently. One very fine painting, to a sympathetic baker.

I heard the click of a tile in the hallway, and the rustle of a dress being stilled by a hand. Cornelia, I thought, still spying. She too is taking her place in the drama.

I waited, holding back the questions I wanted to ask.

Van Leeuwenhoek finally spoke. "Griet, when a will has been drawn up," he began in his deep voice, "an inventory of the family's possessions must be taken to establish the assets while considering the debts. However, there are private matters that Catharina would like to attend to before this is done." He glanced at Catharina. She continued to play with the powder-brush.

They do not like each other still, I thought. They would not even be in the same room together if they could help it.

Van Leeuwenhoek picked up a piece of paper from the table. "He wrote this letter to me ten days before he died," he said to me.

279

He turned to Catharina. "You must do this," he ordered, "for they are yours to give, not his or mine. As executor of his will I should not even be here to witness this, but he was my friend, and I would like to see his wish granted."

Catharina snatched the paper from his hand. "My husband was not a sick man, you know," she addressed herself to me. "He was not really ill until a day or two before his death. It was the strain of the debt that drove him into a frenzy."

I could not imagine my master in a frenzy.

Catharina looked down at the letter, glanced at van Leeuwenhoek, then opened her jewelry box. "He asked that you have these." She picked out the earrings and after a moment's hesitation laid them on the table.

I felt faint and closed my eyes, touching the back of the chair lightly with my fingers to steady myself.

"I have not worn them again," Catharina declared in a bitter tone. "I could not."

I opened my eyes. "I cannot take your earrings, madam."

"Why not? You took them once before. And besides, it's not for you to decide. He has decided for you, and for me. They are yours now, so take them."

I hesitated, then reached over and picked them up. They were cool and smooth to the touch, as I had remembered them, and in their grey and white curve a world was reflected.

I took them.

"Now go," Catharina ordered in a voice muffled with hidden tears. "I have done what he asked. I will do no more." She stood up, crumpled the paper and threw it on the fire. She watched it flare up, her back to me.

I felt truly sorry for her. Although she could not see it, I nodded to her respectfully, and then to van Leeuwenhoek, who smiled at me. "Take care to remain yourself," he had warned me so long ago. I wondered if I had done so. It was not always easy to know.

I slipped across the floor, clutching my earrings, my feet making loose tiles clink together. I closed the door softly behind me.

Cornelia was standing out in the hallway. The brown dress she wore had been repaired in several places and was not as clean as it could be. As I brushed past her she said in a low, eager voice, "You could give them to me." Her greedy eyes were laughing.

I reached over and slapped her.

When I got back to Market Square I stopped by the star in the center and looked down at the pearls in my hand. I could not keep them. What would I do with them? I could not tell Pieter how I came to have them—it would mean explaining everything that had happened so long ago. I could not wear the earrings anyway—a butcher's wife did not wear such things, no more than a maid did.

I walked around the star several times.

Then I set out for a place I had heard of but never been to, tucked away in a back street behind the New Church. I would not have visited such a place ten years before.

The man's trade was keeping secrets. I knew that he would ask me no questions, nor tell anyone that I had gone to him. After seeing so many goods come and go, he was no longer curious about the stories behind them. He held the earrings up to the light, bit them, took them outside to squint at them.

"Twenty guilders," he said.

I nodded, took the coins he held out, and left without looking back.

There were five extra guilders I would not be able to explain. I separated five coins from the others and held them tight in my fist. I would hide them somewhere that Pieter and my sons would not look, some unexpected place that only I knew of.

I would never spend them.

Pieter would be pleased with the rest of the coins, the debt now settled. I would not have cost him anything. A maid came free.

ACKNOWLEDGMENTS

One of the most helpful and readable sources on seventeenth-century Holland is Simon Schama's *The Embarrassment of Riches: An Interpretation of Dutch Culture in the Golden Age* (1987). What little is known about Vermeer's life and family has been thoroughly documented by John Montias in *Vermeer and His Milieu* (1989). The catalogue for the 1996 Vermeer exhibition has beautiful reproductions and clear analyses of the paintings.

I would like to thank Philip Steadman, Nicola Costaras, Humphrey Ocean, and Joanna Woodall for talking with me about various aspects of Vermeer's work. Mick Bartram, Ora Dresner, Nina Killham, Dale Reynolds, and Robert and Angela Royston all made helpful and supportive comments about the manuscript in progress. Thanks, finally, to my agent, Jonny Geller, and my editor, Susan Watt, for doing what they do so well.